THE LITTLE BOOK OF
HORRORS

THE LITTLE BOOK OF
HORRORS

Edited by
SEBASTIAN WOLFE

BARRICADE BOOKS

First published in Great Britain by Xanadu Publications
Limited 1992.
First published in the United States of America by
Barricade Books Inc. 1992, by arrangement with Xanadu
Publications Limited.

Barricade Books Inc.
61 Fourth Avenue, New York, NY 10003
Distributed by Publishers Group West
4065 Hollis, Emeryville, CA 94608

Library of Congress Cataloging-in-Publication Data

The little book of horrors/edited by Sebastian Wolfe
    p.   cm.
  ISBN 0-942637-42-9 : $9.95
  1. Horror tales. 2. Short stories. l. Wolfe, Sebastian
PN6120.95.H727L58   1992   91-29387
808.3'8738—dc20   CIP

Printed in Great Britain

Foreword

The Little Book of Horrors? Tiny Tales of Terror? I will be brief.

It is a book of short-short horror stories, the first of its kind I believe. In it you will find a collection of short, sharp shocks delivered in prose, verse and pictures. Some are blackly humorous, while others are just plain black.

There are tales by such early masters of the form as Ambrose Bierce, Lafcadio Hearn, Charles Dickens and Mark Twain, alongside work by some of the great masters of horror fiction like Robert Bloch and Roald Dahl, and exciting modern writers like Joe R. Lansdale and Richard Christian Matheson.

Among the 'discoveries' are obscure little items by the likes of F. Scott Fitzgerald, Raymond Chandler and Kingsley Amis. By way of contrast, I have also included a selection of 'factual' items, mostly from the old *Police Review*. Cynical readers may find these are fictional as anything else in the book.

The object? To pay tribute to those who have mastered the tricky short-short form, to offer a laugh and a shiver, and to entertain.

Cringe and enjoy.

—S W

CONTENTS

ROALD DAHL
In The Ruins

S omewhere among the bricks and stones, I came across
a man sitting on the ground in his underpants, sawing
off his left leg. There was a black bag beside him, and the
bag was open, and I could see a hypodermic needle lying
there among all the rest of the stuff.

'Do you want some?' he asked, looking up.

'Yes, please,' I said. I was going crazy with hunger.

'I don't mind giving you a bit so long as you will promise
to produce the next meal. I am quite uncontaminated.'

'All right,' I said. 'Yes.'

'Caudal injection,' he said. 'Base of the spine. You don't
feel a thing.'

I found a few bits of wood, and I made a fire in the
ruins, and started roasting a piece of the meat. The doctor
sat on the ground doing things to the stump of his leg.

A child came up, a girl of about four years old. She had
probably seen the smoke from the fire or smelled the smell
of cooking, I don't know which. She was very unsteady on
her feet.

'Do you want some, too?' the doctor asked.

She nodded.

'You'll have to pay it back later,' the doctor said.

The child stood there looking at the piece of meat
that I was holding over the fire on the end of a bent
curtain rod.

'You know something,' the doctor said, 'with all three
of us here, we ought to be able to survive for quite a
long time.'

'I want my mummy,' the child said, starting to cry.

'Sit down,' the doctor told her. 'I'll take care of you.'

JOHN LENNON
Randolf's Party

It was Chrisbus time but Randolph was alone. Where were all his good pals. Bernie, Dave, Nicky, Alice, Beddy, Freba, Viggy, Nigel, Alfred, Clive, Stan, Frenk, Tom, Harry, George, Harold? Where were they on this day? Randolf looged sagely at his only Chrispbut cart from his dad who did not live there.

'I can't understan this being so aloneley on the one day of the year when one would surely spect a pal or two?' thought Rangolf. Hanyway he carried on putting ub the desirations and muzzle toe. All of a surgeon there was amerry timble on the door. Who but who could be a knocking on my door? He open it and there standing there who? but only his pals. Bernie, Dave, Nicky, Alice, Beddy, Freba, Viggy, Nigel, Alfred, Clive, Stan, Frenk, Tom, Harry, George, Harolb weren't they?

Come on in old pals buddys and mates. With a big griff on his face Randoff welcombed them. In they came jorking and labbing shoubing 'Haddy Grimmble, Randoob.' and other hearty, and then they all jumbed on him and did smite him with mighty blows about his head crying, 'We never liked you all the years we've known you. You were never raelly one of us you know, soft head.'

They killed him you know, at least he didn't *die* alone did he? Merry Chrustchove, Randolf old pal buddy.

RICHARD CHRISTIAN MATHESON

Red

He kept walking.

The day was hot and miserable and he wiped his forehead. Up another twenty feet, he could make out more. Thank God. Maybe he'd find it all. He picked up the pace and his breathing got thick. He struggled on, remembering his vow to himself to go through with this, not stopping until he was done. Maybe it had been a mistake to ask this favor. But it was the only way he could think of to work it out. Still, maybe it had been a mistake.

He felt an edge in his stomach as he stopped and leaned down to what was at his feet. He grimaced, lifted it into the large canvas bag he carried, wiped his hands and moved on. The added weight in the bag promised of more and he felt somehow better. He had found most of what he was looking for in the first mile. Only a half more to go, to convince himself, to be sure.

To not go insane.

It was a nightmare for him to realize how far he'd gone this morning with no suspicion, no clue. He held the bag more tightly and walked on. Ahead, the forms who waited got bigger; closer. They stood with arms crossed, people gathered, complaining, behind them.

They would have to wait.

He saw something a few yards up, swallowed and walked closer. It was everywhere and he shut his eyes, trying not to see how it must have been. But he saw it all. Heard it in his head. The sounds were horrible and he couldn't make them go away. Nothing would go away, until he had everything; he was certain of that. Then his mind would at least have some chance to find a place of comfort. To go on.

He bent down and picked up what he could, then walked on, scanning ahead. The sun was beating down and he felt his shirt soaking with sweat under the arms and on his back. He was nearing the forms who waited when he stopped, seeing something halfway between himself and them. It had lost its shape, but he knew what it was and couldn't step any closer. He placed the bag down and slowly sat cross-legged on the baking ground, staring. His body began to shake.

A somber looking man walked to him and carefully picked up the object, placing it in the canvas bag and cinching the top. He gently coaxed the weeping man to stand and the man nodded through tears. Together, they walked toward the others who were glancing at watches and losing patience.

'But I'm not finished,' the man cried. His voice broke and his eyes grew hot and puffy. 'Please . . . I'll go crazy . . . just a little longer?'

The somber looking man hated what was happening and made the decision. 'I'm sorry, sir. Headquarters said I could only give you the half-hour you asked for. That's all I can do. It's a very busy road.'

The man tried to struggle away but was held more tightly. He began to scream and plead and two middle-aged women who were waiting watched uncomfortably.

'Whoever allowed this should be reported,' said one, shaking her head critically. 'The poor man is ready to have a nervous breakdown. It's cruel.'

The other said she'd heard they felt awful for the man, whose little girl had grabbed on when he'd left for work that morning. The girl had gotten caught and he'd never known.

They watched the officer approaching with the crying man who he helped into the hot squad car. Then, the officer grabbed the canvas bag and as it began to drip red onto the blacktop, he gently placed it into the trunk beside the mangled tricycle.

The backed-up cars began to honk and traffic was waved on as the man was driven away.

A WIFE DRIVEN INSANE BY HUSBAND TICKLING HER FEET

On Thursday, last week, a very serious charge was preferred against a man named Michael Puckridge, who resides at Winbursh, a small village in Northumberland. The circumstances, as detailed before the board of guardians, are of a harrowing nature. It appears that Puckridge who has lived very unhappily with his wife, whose life he has threatened on more than one occasion. Most probably he had long contemplated the wicked design which he carried out but too successfully about a fortnight since. Mrs. Puckridge, who is an interesting looking young woman, has for a long time past suffered from varicose veins in the legs, her husband told her that he possessed an infallible remedy for this ailment. **She was induced by her tormentor to**

TICKLEINGAWOMAN'S FEET—A WIFE DRIVEN MAD

allow herself to be tied to a plank, which he placed across two chairs. When the poor woman was bound and helpless, Puckridge deliberately and persistently tickled the soles of her feet with a feather. For a long time he continued to operate upon his unhappy victim, who was rendered frantic by the process.

Eventually she swooned, whereupon her husband released her. It soon became too manifest that the light of reason had fled. Mrs. Puckridge was taken to the workhouse where she was placed with other insane patients. A little girl, a niece of the woman, spoke to one or two of the neighbours saying her aunt had

been tied to a plank and her uncle cruelly illtreated her.

An inquiry was instituted and there is every reason to believe that Mrs. Puckridge had been driven out of her mind in the way described but the result of the investigation is not yet known.

ALEXANDER WOOLLCOTT
Moonlight Sonata

I f this report were to be published in its own England[1], I would
have to cross my fingers in a little foreword explaining that
all the characters were fictitious—which stern requirement of the
British libel law would embarrass me slightly because none of the
character is fictitious, and the story chronicles what, to the best of
my knowledge and belief, actually befell a young English physician
whom I shall call Alvan Barach, because that does not happen to
be his name. It is an account of a hitherto unreported adventure
he had two years ago when he went down into Kent to visit an
old friend—let us call *him* Ellery Cazalet—who spent most of his
days on the links and most of his nights wondering how he would
ever pay the death duties on the collapsing family manor-house to
which he had indignantly fallen heir.

This house was a shabby little cousin to Compton Wynyates, with
roof-tiles of Tudor red making it cosy in the noon-day sun, and a
hoarse bell, which, from the clock tower, had been contemptuously
scattering the hours like coins ever since Henry VIII was a rosy
stripling. Within, Cazalet could afford only a doddering couple to
fend for him, and the once sumptuous gardens did much as they
pleased under the care of a single gardener. I think I must risk giving
the gardener's real name, for none I could invent would have so
appropriate a flavour. It was John Scripture, and he was assisted,
from time to time, by an aged and lunatic father who, in his lucid
intervals, would be let out from his captivity under the eaves of the
lodge to potter amid the lewd topiarian extravagance of the hedges.

The doctor was to come down when he could, with a promise
of some good golf, long nights of exquisite silence, and a ghost or
two thrown in if his fancy ran that way. It was characteristic of his
rather ponderous humour that, in writing to fix a day, he addressed

---

[1]This story was first published in the United States of America.—Ed.

Cazalet at 'The Creeps, Sevenoaks, Kent.' When he arrived, it was to find his host away from home and not due back until all hours. Barach was to dine alone with a reproachful setter for a companion, and not wait up. His bedroom on the ground floor was beautifully panelled from footboard to ceiling, but some misguided housekeeper under the fourth George had fallen upon the lovely woodwork with a can of black varnish. The dowry brought by a Cazalet bride of the mauve decade had been invested in a few vintage bathrooms, and one of these had replaced a prayer closet that once opened into this bedroom. There was only a candle to read by, but the light of a full moon came waveringly through the wind-stirred vines that half curtained the mullioned windows.

In this museum, Barach dropped off to sleep. He did not know how long he had slept when he found himself awake again, and conscious that something was astir in the room. It took him a moment to place the movement, but at last, in a patch of moonlight, he made out a hunched figure that seemed to be sitting with bent, engrossed head in the chair by the door. It was the hand, or the the whole arm, that was moving, tracing a recurrent if irregular course in the air. At first the gesture was teasingly half-familiar, and then Barach recognized it as the one a woman makes when embroidering. There would be a hesitation as if the needle were being thrust through some taut, resistant material, and then, each time, the long, swift sure pull of the thread.

To the startled guest, this seemed the least menacing activity he had ever heard ascribed to a ghost, but just the same he had only one idea, and that was to get out of that room with all possible dispatch. His mind made a hasty reconnaissance. The door into the hall was out of the question, for madness lay that way. At least he would have to pass right by that weaving arm. Nor did he relish a blind plunge into the thorny shrubbery beneath his window, and a barefoot scamper across the frosty turf. Of course, there was the bathroom, but that was small comfort if he could not get out of it by another door. In a spasm of concentration, he remembered that he *had* seen another door. Just at the moment of this realization, he heard the comfortingly actual sound of a car coming up the drive, and guessed that it was his host returning. In one magnificent movement, he leaped to the floor, bounded into the bathroom, and bolted its door behind him. The floor of the room beyond was quilted with moonlight. Wading through that, he arrived breathless, but unmolested, in the corridor. Further along he could see the lamp left burning in the entrance hall and hear the clatter of his host closing the front door.

As Barach came hurrying out of the darkness to greet him, Cazalet boomed his delight at such affability, and famished by his long, cold ride, proposed an immediate raid on the larder. The doctor, already sheepish at his recent panic, said nothing about it, and was all for food at once. With lighted candles held high, the foraging party descended on the offices, and mine host was descanting on the merits of cold roast beef, Cheddar cheese, and milk as a light midnight snack, when he stumbled over a bundle on the floor. With a cheerful curse at the old goody of the kitchen who was always leaving something about, he bent to see what it was this time, and let out a whistle of surprise. Then, by two candles held low, he and the doctor saw something they will not forget while they live. It was the body of the cook. Just the body. The head was gone. On the floor alongside lay a bloody cleaver.

'Old Scripture, by God!' Cazalet cried out, and, in a flash, Barach guessed. Still clutching a candle in one hand, he dragged his companion back through the interminable house to the room from which he had fled, motioning him to be silent, tiptoeing the final steps. The precaution was wasted, for a regiment could not have disturbed the rapt contentment of the ceremony still in progress within. The old lunatic had not left his seat by the door. Between his knees he still held the head of the woman he had killed. Scrupulously, happily, crooning at his work, he was plucking out the grey hairs one by one.

ALISTAIR SAMPSON
(Untitled)

I've just acquired some shrunken heads
To pop in other people's beds.
Some are really frightfully small
And some have hardly shrunk at all.
Tell me, which is your divan?
I'll pop a head in if I can.

17

"*This particular gem has an interesting curse attached to it . . .!*"

GEORGE D PAINTER
Meeting with a Double

When George began to climb all unawares
He saw a horrible face at the top of the stairs.

The rats came tumbling down the planks,
Pushing past without a word of thanks.

The rats were thin, the stairs were tall,
But the face at the top was worst of all.

It wasn't the ghost of his father or mother.
When they are laid there's always another.

It wasn't the ghost of people he knew.
It was worse than this, shall I tell you who?

It was himself, oh, what a disgrace.
And soon they were standing face to face.

At first they pretended neither cared,
But whe they met, they stood and stared.

One started to smile and the other to frown.
And one moved up and the other moved down.

But which emerged and which one stays,
Nobody will know till the end of his days.

AMBROSE BIERCE
John Mortonson's Funeral

John Mortonson was dead: his lines in 'the tragedy of "Man"', had all been spoken and he had left the stage. The body rested in a fine mahogany coffin fitted with a plate of glass. All arrangements for the funeral had been so well attended to that had the deceased known he would doubtless have approved. The face, as it showed under the glass, was not disagreeable to look upon: it bore a faint smile, and as the death had been painless, had not been distorted beyond the repairing power of the undertaker. At two o'clock of the afternoon the friends were to assemble to pay their last tribute of respect to one who had no further need of friends and respect. The surviving members of the family came severally every few minutes to the casket and wept above the placid features beneath the glass. This did them no good; it did no good to John Mortonson; but in the presence of death reason and philosophy are silent.

As the hour of two approached the friends began to arrive and after offering such consolation to the stricken relatives as the proprieties of the occasion required, solemnly seated themselves about the room with an augmented consciousness of their importance in the scheme funereal. Then the minister came, and in that overshadowing presence the lesser lights went into eclipse. His entrance was followed by that of the widow, whose lamentations filled the room. She approached the casket and after leaning her face against the cold glass for a moment was gently led to a seat near her daughter. Mournfully and low the man of God began his eulogy of the dead, and his doleful voice, mingled with the sobbing which it was its purpose to stimulate and sustain, rose and fell, seemed to come and go, like the sound of a sullen sea. The gloomy day grew darker as he spoke; a curtain of cloud underspread the sky and a few drops of rain fell audibly. It seemed as if all nature were weeping for John Mortonson.

When the minister had finished his eulogy with prayer a hymn was sung and the pallbearers took their places beside the bier. As the last notes of the hymn died away the widow ran to the coffin, cast herself upon it and sobbed hysterically. Gradually, however, she yielded to dissuasion, becoming more composed; and as the minister was in the act of leading her away her eyes sought the face of the dead beneath the glass. She threw up her arms and with a shriek fell backward insensible.

The mourners sprang forward to the coffin, the friends followed, and as the clock on the mantel solemnly struck three all were staring down upon the face of John Mortonson, deceased.

They turned away, sick and faint. One man, trying in his terror to escape the awful sight, stumbled against the coffin so heavily as to knock away one of its frail supports. The coffin fell to the floor, the glass was shattered to bits by the concussion.

From the opening crawled John Mortonson's cat, which lazily leapt to the floor, sat up, tranquilly wiped its crimson muzzle with a forepaw, then walked with dignity from the room.

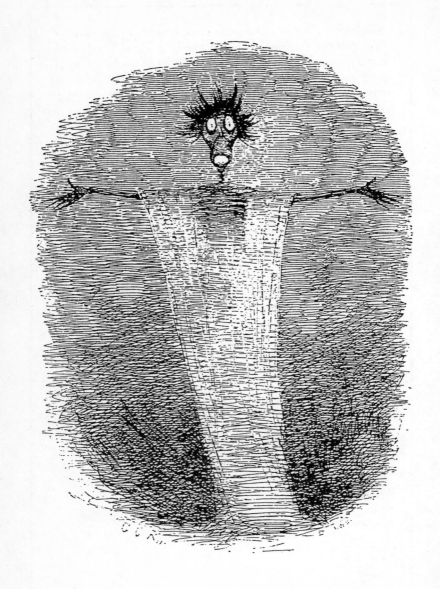

E.H. VISIAK

The Skeleton at the Feast

Dance in the wind, poor skeleton!
 You that was my deary one,
You they hanged for stealing sheep.
Dance and dangle, laugh and leap!
Tomorrow night at Squire's ball,
I am to serve a sheep in hall:
My Lady's wedding, Lord love her!
Wait until they lift the cover!

ORNELLA VOLTA
(Untitled)

Doctor Craven examined the case of a thirty year old Portuguese who, according to him, had the viscid eyes and movements of a reptile:

'The thoughts and fantasies of the subject all moved around the idea of blood, which she expressed by means of bloodthirsty metaphors and symbols. Blood for her is the symbol of love, hate, anger, and passion. She wants to know in what way human blood is different from animals' blood and has set herself this problem: what aspect would blood have if it were to lose its colour? What would be the appearance of a body deprived of its vital liquid? Would it be pale and cold? Would it diminish in size? When it rains, she imagines that it is raining blood and the mere idea of blood dripping from a disintegrating cloud in a completely clear sky sends her into ecstasy. She likes to suck and swallow blood, but does not dare to do so, for fear of making its owner suffer. She drinks red wine only because it has the colour of blood and, for the same reason, likes blood oranges.

'She has the habit of mentally amusing herself with images of foetuses and corpses of mammals. She thinks she hates her little seven year old boy because he does not resemble her husband. The hate the child inspires in her has led her to entertain homicidal desires from time to time. She would then like to kill him, not with a knife, but by breaking his neck with her own two hands. Moreover, she has experienced the same homicidal impulses towards her husband. She would like to do away with him, strangling him and keeping his corpse in her bedroom.

'She would also like to dispose of her father's body and, if she could touch her mother's skull with her hand she would be infinitely happy. She also makes plans regarding the eventual use of the corpse of her husband and the two children. She would like to eat their flesh, without swallowing it and raw, of course, so as not to lose the flavour of the blood.

'Instead of a true and proper sexual union, she greatly prefers to suck the blood of her partner from a little hole made in the cavity of his ear. During the orgasm she seems to die and she then remains immobile like a corpse.'

COLIN WEST
Cousin Jane

Yesterday my cousin Jane
Said she was an aeroplane,
But I wanted further proof –
So I pushed her off the roof.

ALISTAIR SAMPSON
(Untitled)

'I have a man at last,' she cried
And the party glasses clinked.
'You have a man?' aghast they cried –
And everybody winked.

'He's strong and fair and debonair,
Tanned from a life in the open air,
Six feet five and a quarter.'
'It might be best,' said a friendly guest
'If you added a drop more water.'

'You are all of you quite out-classed,' she cried,
'He is lying on my bed.'
'Make that drink your last,' they cried,
'Here's orange-juice instead.'

'He's mine, all mine, and quite divine,
None of you ever had men so fine,
And he's six feet six – or nearly.
He's fast asleep, so go and peep
At the man that I love so dearly.'

'She HAS a man at last,' they cried –
'He's lying on her bed –
He's a handsome man,' aghast they cried,
'But we're fairly sure he's dead.'

JEFFRY SCOTT
Out of the Country

M r. Billy Bullivant's baby-blue eyes twinkled ingratiatingly as he set the murderer at ease. 'You'll be out of the country by this time tomorrow,' he promised, 'with no trouble at all. My system's foolproof, I assure you.'

'It's damned expensive, too,' grunted the visitor.

An expression of near consternation flitted across Mr. Bullivant's bland, creaseless pink face. 'Oh dear, don't tell me you haven't got enough money. That would be too bad.'

The murderer chuckled without humour, flicking open a cigarette case which had cost more than Mr. Bullivant spent on tobacco in a year. 'Set your mind at rest, I'm not down to my last thousand yet.'

The heavy furrows running from domineering nose to lantern jaw deepened suddenly. 'Look here, Bullivant, this swanning off into the blue business just won't do. I've got a definite objective in mind, and since I'm paying this much, I might as well go straight there.'

Mr. Billy Bullivant stared back owlishly for a moment. Then he opened a drawer in his desk and dropped a late-city edition of the evening paper on the scarred and tea-ringed wood. 'The police have a definite objective in mind for you, too,' he said flatly.

It became evident that he was neither childish nor soft.

'You might have done me the favour of crediting me with a little intelligence, you know. "*Tax troubles*", you reckoned, when you phoned this afternoon. Wife troubles would be nearer the mark – and what a messy solution you found.'

In the silence which followed, they could hear the dreary call of a ship leaving harbour, and the dried-leaf rustling of rats in the factory beneath the stuffy little office.

'I – I'm sorry,' said the murderer, stupidly. Then, as he recovered: 'But where *are* you sending me?'

'It depends, ol' man.' Mr. Bullivant pursed his lips and squinted judicially. 'I'll just scan the orders I get in the morning, you see, and push you off with the next consignment to whatever spot happens to be furthest away.'

The murderer swallowed drily. 'Sounds . . . uncomfortable,' he muttered. And lit another cigarette.

'You won't feel a thing,' joked Mr. Bullivant.

Climbing wearily up the stairs to the office in the early hours of the following morning, a ghost of golden stubble sanding his plump chops, he discovered the factory cat stretched on its side, legs stiff and jaws frozen in a maniac grin. The overturned glass opposite Mr. Bullivant's own on the desk gave a clue to the small tragedy.

His mild eyes misted. But even in his sorrow he reflected on how much the cat resembled the murderer – and vice versa. Not surprising, since they had both sipped the same final drink.

Stopping only to take a fat cigarette from his newly-acquired gold case, Mr. Bullivant plodded downstairs with the little corpse wrapped in the previous evening's paper.

'Woman found dead in flat. Man sought by police,' screamed the headlines on the newsprint shroud.

'Dead as yesterday's news – what an apt phrase,' muttered Mr. Bullivant as he passed the sizeable pile of dog-food tins which he had filled during the night.

Gaudy labels bore a modest message: *Bullivant's Mystery Mixture * * * British and Best * * * Made By Men Who Love Dogs, To a Centuries-old Recipe.*

Mr. Bullivant's habitual good humour came to the surface once more and, shifting the grim parcel to his left hand, he gave the nearest tin an approving pat. In a few days the consignment would be on its way to the United States, a hundred tins among two thousand.

Or had the latest order come from Paris? No matter, thought Mr. Bullivant, with a shrug. One of his aged, not-too-bright work-people would sort it out when they came in.

The important thing was that a contract had been honoured.

Mr. Bullivant's murderer – his latest murderer – was getting out of the country.

STEPHEN GALLAGHER
Mousetrap

'This wasn't where I'd asked to go,' the woman told me. I'd been walking the streets for hours, now, and she was the first sign of life that I'd seen. Every house stood empty – perfect outside, a ruin within.

'A red taxi?' I said.

She nodded. 'I didn't see the driver.'

Lights came on at dusk, shining in rooms where nobody walked. We found bones in cellars, half-hidden abandoned cars; something had devoured the town and then somehow left it running as a lure for others.

'There's no way out,' she said.

'Correct,' I said. And then I ate her.

SINGULAR METHOD OF EXECUTION

A strange and dreadful mode of executing criminals exists in Persia. The Shah is supposed to witness these executions. "During my stay in Teheran" says Mr. Fowler, in his interesting work, "a culprit was suspended by the legs from two poles, and literally cut in half by the henchman in the royal presence.

"This mode of punishment is common in Persia, and it is called the 'shekeh', and is performed by the chief executioner, a most important officer, and always His Majesty's person.

"They sometimes adopt the ancient method of execution, said to have been first tried upon Bessus, the murderer of Darius—that of having two young trees brought together by main strength at their summits, and then fastened with cords. The culprit being brought out and his legs tied with ropes at the top of the trees, the cords which fasten them together are then cut, and by the power and elasticity of their spring the body of the culprit is immediately torn asunder, and the different parts are left attached to each tree separately."

ROBERT BLOCH
The Model Wife

M urder, like love, is blind. It knows neither color nor creed.
　　Elise, for example, was a quadroon, and although she was perhaps the most beautiful member of the *demi-monde* in all Haiti, she was a devout churchgoer.

Josef was a mulatto and, despite his education, not a communicant of any established religion. Although he held a reputable position as display manager for the leading department store in Port-au-Prince, he came originally from the hill country where voodoo still flourishes.

Elise had *her* particular reputation, yet she gave up a promising career to marry Josef. And Josef, who some had predicted might have developed his native talent as a brilliant artist and sculptor, contented himself instead with routine commercial employment in order to support his voluptuous young bride.

They made a somewhat incongruous couple, but for a while all went happily.

Yet in the end, as the old saying goes, blood will tell. Elise was civilized, and Josef was still a savage.

Because Elise was civilized, she fell in love with Monsieur Carnet. Monsieur Carnet was an octoroon, and quite wealthy. He wanted to take her with him to Paris. 'A wonderful life awaits you, *cherie*,' he told her. 'You will pass for white easily enough, just as I do. France is a civilized country. I have means, we will travel, you shall be able to do all the things you were meant to enjoy—'

Because Josef was a savage, he did not understand all this, even though Elise carefully explained what such an opportunity meant to her.

For a short time, therefore—because *she* was civilized—Elise toyed with the idea that she might have to kill Josef in order to be free of him.

But in the end—because he was a savage—Josef relapsed into a sullen silence and let her go. He did not attempt to interfere with her meetings with Monsieur Carnet, and he did not contest the divorce proceedings. A month later, Elise sailed away with her new protector.

Before sailing, it is probable that she prayed to her God, just as it is unmistakable that Josef prayed to his. Yet, in the end, she left.

Elise and Monsieur Carnet planned to be married on shipboard, en route to France, and a gala ceremony had been arranged. Unfortunately, on the second day of the voyage she became ill. It was an illness which baffled the ship's doctor.

When the fever came, early that morning, Elise complained that she was burning up. Within an hour she was screaming in agony. They packed her beautiful body in cold sheets moistened with water, but she continued to writhe in torment, and no amount of morphine could dull the pain.

No amount of morphine could dull the shock of witnessing her rapid and incredible disintegration—the way the flesh seemed to literally melt from her face and body. In the end there was only a bubbling, coagulated horror.

It was not a civilized way in which to die, but then Josef was a savage. And although he was never formally indicted for murder, he did suffer some consequences. In fact, that very day, he lost his job as display manager of Port-au-Prince's leading department store.

They could not understand why a man of his experience would insist on making a window dummy of his own to place on display that morning. They could not see why he modeled the face and features to an uncanny resemblance of his former wife. And above all, they could not comprehend why he chose to mold the dummy of soft wax—wax that was bound to melt and run after an hour or so in the hot sun.

JOHN LENNON
Good dog Nigel

A rf, Arf, he goes, a merry sight,
 Our little hairy friend,
Arf, Arf, upon the lampost bright
Arfing round the bend.
Nice dog! Goo boy,
Waggie tail and beg,
Clever Nigel, jump for joy
Because we're putting you to sleep at three of the clock,
Nigel.

JOE R. LANSDALE
Dog, Cat, and Baby

Dog did not like Baby. For that matter, Dog did not like Cat. But Cat had claws – sharp claws.

Dog had always gotten attention. Pat on head. 'Here, boy, here's a treat. Nice dog. Good dog. Shake hands. Speak! Sit. Nice dog.'

Now there was Baby.

Cat had not been problem, really.

Cat was liked, not loved by family. They petted Cat sometimes. Fed her. Did not mistreat her. But they not love her. Not way they loved Dog – before Baby.

Damn little pink thing that cried.

Baby got 'Oooohs and Ahhhs.' When Dog tried to get close to Masters, they say, 'Get back, boy. Not *now*.'

When would be *now*?

Dog never see now. Always Baby get now. Dog get nothing. Sometimes they so busy with Baby it be all day before dog get fed. Dog never get treats anymore. Could not remember last pat on head or 'Good Dog!'

Bad business. Dog not like it.

Dog decide to do something about it.

Kill Baby. Then there be Dog, Cat again. They not love Cat, so things be okay.

Dog thought that over. Wouldn't take much to rip little Baby apart. Baby soft, pink. Would bleed easy.

Baby often put in Jumper which hung between doorway when Master Lady hung wash. Baby be easy to get then.

So Dog waited.

One day Baby put in Jumper and Master Lady go outside to hang out wash. Dog looks at pink thing jumping, thinks about ripping to pieces. Thinks on it long and hard. Thought makes him so happy his mouth drips water. Dog starts toward Baby, making fine moment last.

Baby looks up, sees Dog coming toward it slowly, almost creeping. Baby starts to cry.

But before Dog can reach Baby, Cat jumps.

Cat been hiding behind couch.

Cat goes after Dog, tears Dog's face with teeth, with claws. Dog bleeds, tries to run. Cat goes after him.

Dog turns to bite.

Cat hangs claw in Dog's eye.

Dog yelps, runs.

Cat jumps on Dog's back, biting Dog on top of head.

Dog tries to turn corner into bedroom. Cat, tearing at him with claws, biting with teeth, makes Dog lose balance. Dog running very fast, fast as he can go, hits the edge of doorway, stumbles back, falls over.

Cat gets off Dog.

Dog lies still.

Dog not breathing.

Cat knows Dog is dead. Cat licks blood from claws, from teeth with rough tongue.

Cat has gotten rid of Dog.

Cat turns to look down hall where Baby is screaming. Now for *other* one.

Cat begins to creep down hall.

The Nun is fearfully bedevilled:
She runs about and moans and shrieks;
Her flesh is bruised, her clothes dishevelled:
She's been like this for weeks and weeks.

– Edward Gorey

KINGSLEY AMIS
Mason's Life

'**M**ay I join you?'
The medium-sized man with the undistinguished clothes
and the blank, anonymous face looked up at Pettigrew, who, glass
of beer in hand, stood facing him across the small corner table.
Pettigrew, tall, handsome and of fully-moulded features, had about
him an intent, almost excited air that, in different circumstances,
might have brought an unfavourable response, but the other said
amiably,

'By all means. Do sit down.'

'Can I get you something?'

'No, I'm fine, thank you,' said the medium-sized man, gesturing
at the almost-full glass in front of him. In the background was
the ordinary ambience of bar, barman, drinkers in ones and twos,
nothing to catch the eye.

'We've never met, have we?'

'Not as far as I recall.'

'Good, good. My name's Pettigrew, Daniel R. Pettigrew. What's
yours?'

'Mason. George Herbert Mason, if you want it in full.'

'Well, I think that's best, don't you? George . . . Herbert . . .
Mason.' Pettigrew spoke as if committing the three short words to
memory. 'Now let's have your telephone number.'

Again Mason might have reacted against Pettigrew's demanding
manner, but he said no more than, 'You can find me in the book
easily enough.'

'No, there might be several . . . We mustn't waste time. Please.'

'Oh, very well; it's public information, after all. Two-three-two,
five—'

'Hold on, you're going too fast for me. Two . . . three . . .
two . . .'

'Five-four-five-four.'

'What a stroke of luck. I ought to be able to remember that.'

'Why don't you write it down if it's so important to you?'

At this, Pettigrew gave a knowing grin that faded into a look of disappointment. 'Don't you know that's no use? Anyway: two-three-two, five-four-five-four. I might as well give you my number too. Seven—'

'I don't want your number, Mr. Pettigrew,' said Mason, sounding a little impatient, 'and I must say I rather regret giving you mine.'

'But you must take my number.'

'Nonsense; you can't make me.'

'A phrase, then – let's agree on a phrase to exchange in the morning.'

'Would you mind telling me what this is all about?'

'Please, our time's running out.'

'You keep saying that. Our time for what?'

'Any moment everything might change and I might find myself somewhere completely different, and so might you, I suppose, though I can't help feeling it's doubtful whether—'

'Mr. Pettigrew, either you explain yourself at once or I'll have you removed.'

'All right,' said Pettigrew, whose disappointed look had deepened, 'but I'm afraid it won't do any good. You see, when we started talking I thought you must be a real person, because of the way you—'

'Spare me your infantile catch-phrases, for heaven's sake. So I'm not a real person,' cooed Mason offensively.

'I don't mean it like that, I mean it in the most literal way possible.'

'Oh, God. Are you mad or drunk or what?'

'Nothing like that. I'm asleep.'

'Asleep?' Mason's nondescript face showed total incredulity.

'Yes. As I was saying, at first I took you for another real person in the same situation as myself: sound asleep, dreaming, aware of the fact, and anxious to exchange names and telephone numbers and so forth with the object of getting in touch the next day and confirming the shared experience. That would prove something remarkable about the mind, wouldn't it? – people communicating via their dreams. It's a pity one so seldom realises one's dreaming: I've only been able to try the experiment four or five times in the last twenty years, and I've never had any success. Either I forget the details or I find there's no such person, as in this case. But I'll go on—'

'You're sick.'

'Oh no. Of course it's conceivable there is such a person as you. Unlikely, though, or you'd have recognized the true situation at once, I feel, instead of arguing against it like this. As I say, I may be wrong.'

'It's hopeful that you say that.' Mason had calmed down, and lit a cigarette with deliberation. 'I don't know much about these things, but you can't be too far gone if you admit you could be in error. Now let me just assure you that I didn't come into existence five minutes ago inside your head. My name, as I told you, is George Herbert Mason. I'm forty-six years old, married, three children, job in the furniture business . . . Oh hell, giving you no more than an outline of my life so far would take all night, as it would in the case of anybody with an average memory. Let's finish our drinks and go along to my house, and then we can—'

'You're just a man in my dream saying that,' said Pettigrew loudly. 'Two-three-two, five-four-five-four. I'll call the number if it exists, but it won't be you at the other end. Two-three-two—'

'Why are you so agitated, Mr. Pettigrew?'

'Because of what's going to happen to you at any moment.'

'What can happen to me? Is this a threat?'

Pettigrew was breathing fast. His finely-drawn face began to coarsen, the pattern of his jacket to become blurred. 'The telephone!' he shouted. 'It must be later than I thought!'

'Telephone?' repeated Mason, blinking and screwing up his eyes as Pettigrew's form continued to change.

'The one at my bedside! I'm waking up!'

Mason grabbed the other by the arm, but that arm had lost the greater part of its outline, had become a vague patch of light already fading, and when Mason looked at the hand that had done the grabbing, his own hand, he saw with difficulty it likewise no longer had fingers, or front or back, or skin, or anything.

WILLIAM PLOMER
The Dorking Thigh

About to marry and invest
　　Their lives in safety and routine
Stanley and June required a nest
And came down on the 4.15.

The agent drove them to the Posh Estate
And showed them several habitations.
None did. The afternoon got late
With questions, doubts, and explanations.

Then day grew dim and Stan fatigued
And disappointment raised its head,
But June declared herself intrigued
To know where that last turning led.

It led to a Tudor snuggery styled
'Ye Kumfi Nooklet' on the gate.
'A gem of a home,' the salesman smiled,
'My pet place on the whole estate;

'It's not quite finished, but you'll see
Good taste itself.' They went inside.
'This little place is built to be
A husband's joy, a housewife's pride.'

They saw the white convenient sink,
The modernistic chimneypiece,
June gasped for joy, Stan gave a wink
To say, 'Well, here our quest can cease.'

The salesman purred (he'd managed well)
And June undid a cupboard door.
'For linen,' she beamed. And out there fell
A nameless Something on the floor.

'Something the workman left, I expect,'
The agent said, as it fell at his feet,
Nor knew that his chance of a sale was wrecked.
'Good heavens, it must be a joint of meat!'

Ah yes, it was meat, it was meat all right,
A joint those three will never forget—
For they stood alone in the Surrey night
With the severed thigh of a plump brunette ...

Early and late, early and late,
Traffic was jammed round the Posh Estate,
And the papers were full of the Dorking Thigh
And who, and when, and where, and why.

A trouser button was found in the mud.
(Who made it? Who wore it? Who lost it? Who knows?)
But no one found a trace of blood
Or her body or face, or the spoiler of those.

He's acting a play in the common air
On which no curtain can ever come down.
Though 'Ye Kumfi Nooklet' was shifted elsewhere
June made Stan take a flat in town.

ORNELLA VOLTA
Henri Blot (Fact)

Tried in Paris in 1886 for violation of graves, thus described by a witness: 'He is twenty-six years old and rather handsome despite his livid complexion. He wears a forelock of hair over his forehead *à la chien* and his moustaches are well trimmed at the sides. His eyes are a dark black and strikingly sunk in his orbits and he has the habit of often fluttering his eyelids. There is something feline about his physiognomy, and at the same time he makes one think of a hawk.'

He only violated two corpses, both at the cemetery of Saint-Ouen: one belonged to the performer Fernande Méry, known as Carmanio, and the other was that of a one-year-old child. Before committing his violations, he always placed some sheets of vellum paper under his knees which he had taken from bunches of flowers on tombs, as 'a precaution'. Each time he had finished his act he had the misfortune of falling asleep on the spot and was therefore caught on his second attempt.

See: Albert Bataille, *Les Causes criminelles et mondaines*, Paris, 1886.

CHARLES DICKENS
Captain Murderer

The first diabolical character who intruded himself on my peaceful youth was a certain Captain Murderer. This wretch must have been an offshoot of the Blue Beard family, but I head no suspicion of the consanguinity in those times. His warning name would seem to have awakened no general prejudice against him, for he was admitted into the best society and possessed immense wealth. Captain Murderer's mission was matrimony, and the gratification of a cannibal appetite with tender brides. On his marriage morning, he always caused both sides of the way to church to be planted with curious flowers; and when his bride said, 'Dear Captain Murderer, I never saw flowers like these before: what are they called?' he answered, 'They are called Garnish for house-lamb,' and laughed at his ferocious practical joke in a horrid manner, disquieting the minds of the noble bridal company, with a very sharp show of teeth, then displayed for the first time. He made love in a coach and six, and married in a coach and twelve, and all his horses were milk-white horses with one red spot on the back which he caused to be hidden by the harness. For, the spot *would* come there, though every horse was milk-white when Captain Murderer bought him. And the spot was young bride's blood. (To this terrific point I am indebted for my first personal experience of a shudder and cold beads on the forehead.) When Captain Murderer had made an end of feasting and revelry, and had dismissed the noble guests, and was alone with his wife on the day month after their marriage, it was his whimsical custom to produce a golden rolling-pin and a silver pie-board. Now, there was the special feature in the Captain's courtships, that he always asked if the young lady could make pie-crust; and if she couldn't by nature or education, she was taught. Well. When the bride saw Captain Murderer produce the golden rolling-pin and silver pie-board, she remembered this, and turned up her laced-silk sleeves to make a pie. The Captain brought out a silver pie-dish

43

of immense capacity, and the Captain brought out flour and butter and eggs and all things needful, except the inside of the pie; of materials for the staple of the pie itself, the Captain brought out none. Then said the lovely bride, 'Dear Captain Murderer, what pie is this to be?' He replied, 'A meat pie.' Then said the lovely bride, 'Dear Captain Murderer, I see no meat.' The Captain humourously retorted, 'Look in the glass.' She looked in the glass, but still she saw no meat, and then the Captain roard with laughter, and suddenly frowning and drawing his sword, bade her roll out the crust. So she rolled out the crust, dropping large tears upon it all the time because he was so cross, and when she had lined the dish with crust and had cut the crust all ready to fit the top, the Captain called out, '*I see the meat in the glass!*' And the bride looked up at the glass, just in time to see the Captain cutting her head off; and he chopped her in pieces, and peppered her, and salted her, and put her in the pie, and sent it to the baker's and ate it all, and picked the bones.

Captain Murderer went on in this way, prospering exceedingly, until he came to choose a bride from two twin sisters, and at first didn't know which to choose. For, though one was fair and the other dark, they were both equally beautiful. But the fair twin loved him, and the dark twin hated him, so he chose the fair one. The dark twin would have prevented the marriage if she could, but she couldn't; however, on the night before it, much suspecting Captain Murderer, she stole out and climbed his garden wall, and looked in at his window through a chink in the shutter, and saw him having his teeth filed sharp. Next day she listened all day, and heard him make his joke about the house-lamb. And that day month, he had the paste rolled out, and cut the fair twin's head off, and chopped her in pieces, and peppered her, and salted her, and put her in the pie, and sent it to the baker's, and ate it all, and picked the bones.

Now, the dark twin had had her suspicions much increased by the filing of the Captain's teeth, and again by the houselamb joke. Putting all things together when he gave out that her sister was dead, she divined the truth, and determined to be revenged. So, she went up to Captain Murderer's house, and knocked at the knocker and pulled at the bell, and when the Captain came to the door, said: 'Dear Captain Murderer, marry me next, for I always loved you and was jealous of my sister.' The Captain took it as a compliment and made a polite answer, and the marriage was quickly arranged.

On the night before it, the bride again climbed to his window, and again saw him having his teeth filed sharp. At this sight she laughed such a terrible laugh at the chink in the shutter, that the Captain's blood curdled, ad he said: 'I hope nothing has disagreed with me!' At that, she laughed again, a still more terrible laugh, and the shutter was opened and search made, but she was nimbly gone, and there was no one. Next day they went to church in a coach and twelve, and were married. And that day month, she rolled the pie-crust out, and Captain Murderer cut her head off, and chopped her in pieces, and peppered her and salted her, and put her in the pie, and sent it to the baker's, and ate it all, and picked the bones.

But before she began to roll out the paste she had taken a deadly poison of a most awful character, distilled from toads' eyes and spiders' knees; and Captain Murderer had hardly picked her last bone, when he began to swell, and turn blue, and to be all over spots, and to scream. And he went on swelling and turning bluer, and being more all over spots and screaming, until he reached from floor to ceiling and from wall to wall; and then, at one o'clock in the morning, he blew up with a loud explosion. At the sound of it, all the milk-white horses in the stables broke their halters and went mad, and then they galloped over everybody in Captain Murderer's house (beginning with the family blacksmith who had filed his teeth) until the whole were dead, and then they galloped away.

F SCOTT FITZGERALD
(Untitled)

In a dear little vine covered cottage
    On Forty-second Street
A butcher once did live who dealt
    In steak and other meat

His son was very nervous
    And his mother him did vex
And she failed to make allowance
    For his matricide complex
    And now in old Sing Sing
    You can hear that poor lad sing

Just a boy that killed his mother
    I was always up to tricks
When she taunted me I shot her
    Through her chronic appendix
I was always very nervous
    And it really isn't fair
I bumped off my mother but never no other
    Will you let me die in the chair?

II

He was only sixteen and a fraction
    A had ne'er been ail in his life
He had scarcely been fired from his high school
    For raping the principal's wife

Now he sits in the laws foulest dungeons
    Instead of his families embrace
Oh how would you like it your ownself
    If you stared the hot seat in the face
    So write Franklin D. if you can
    To send him to old Mattewan
Just a boy that killed his mother
    Now he's in a sorry fix
Since he up one day and plugged her
    Through her perfect thirty-six
It was no concern of no one's
    And his trial wasn't fair
The fact that he shot her was a family matter
    Will you let him die in the chair?

III

Do you think that our civilization
    Should punish an innocent lad
Why he said to the judge in the court room
    He was aiming the gun at his dad

But the judges denied his petition
    And at dawn on the 9th of July
Unless Governor Roosevelt shows kindness
    Gus Schnlitski must certainly die
And the death house once again
    Does ring to this refrain
Just a boy that killed his mother
    With a brace of stolen colts
On July 9 they'll fill me
    With a hundred thousand volts
It was dope that made me do it
    Otherwise I wouldn't dare
'Twas ten grains of morphine that made me an orphinc
    Will you let me die in the chair?

48

JOE R. LANSDALE

Chompers

O ld Maude, who lived in alleys, combed trash cans, and picked rags, found the false teeth in a puddle of blood back of Denny's. Obvious thing was that there had been a mugging, and some unfortunate who'd been wandering around out back had gotten his or her brains beaten out, and then hauled off somewhere for who knows what.

But the teeth, which had probably hopped from the victim's mouth like some kind of frightened animal, still remained, and the bloody they lay in was testimony to the terrible event.

Maude picked them up, looked at them. Besides the blood there were some pretty nasty coffee stains on the rear molars and what looked to be a smidgen of cherry pie. One thing Maude could spot and tell with an amazing degree of accuracy was a stain or a food dollop. Cruise alleyways and dig in trash cans most of your life, and you get skilled.

Now, Maude was a practical old girl, and, as she had about as many teeth in her head as a pomegranate, she wiped the blood off on her dress—high fashion circa 1920—and put those suckers right square in her gummy little mouth. Somehow it seemed like the proper thing to do.

Perfect fit. Couldn't have been any better than if they'd been made for her. She got the old, blackened lettuce head out of her carpet bag—she'd found the lettuce with a half a tomato back of Burger King—and gave that vegetable a chomp. Sounded like the dropping of a guillotine as those teeth snapped into the lettuce and then ground it to smithereens.

Man, that was good for a change, thought Maude, to be able to go at your food like a pig to trough. Gumming your vittles gets old.

The teeth seemed a little tighter in her mouth than a while ago, but Maude felt certain that after a time she'd get used to them. It was sad about the poor soul that had lost them, but that person's bad luck was her fortune.

Maude started toward the doorway she called home, and by the time she'd gone a block she found that she was really hungry, which surprised her. Not an hour back she'd eaten half a hamburger out of a Burger King trash can, three greasy fries, and half an apple pie. But, boy howdy, did she want to chow down now. She felt like she could eat anything.

She got the tomato half out of her bag, along with everything else in there that looked edible, and began to eat.

More she ate, hungrier she got. Pretty soon she was out of goodies, and the sidewalk and the street started looking to her like the bottom of a dinner plate that ought to be filled. God, but her belly burned. It was as if she'd never eaten and had suddenly become aware of the need.

She ground her big teeth and walked on. Half a block later she spotted a big alleycat hanging head down over the lip of a trash can, pawing for something to eat, and ummm, ummm, ummm, but that cat looked tasty as a Dunkin' Donut.

Chased that rascal for three blocks, but didn't catch it. It pulled a fade-out on her in a dark alley.

Disgusted, but still very, very hungry, Maude left the alley thinking: Chow, need me some chow.

Beat cop, O'Hara, was twirling his nightstick when he saw her nibbling the paint of a rusty old streetlamp. It was an old woman with a prune face, and when he came up she stopped nibbling and looked at him. She had the biggest shiniest pair of choppers he had ever seen. They stuck out from between her lips like a gator's teeth, and in the light of the streetlamp, even as he watched, he thought for a moment that he had seen them grow. And, by golly, they looked pointed now.

O'Hara had walked his beat for twenty years, and he was used to eccentrics and weird getups, but there was something particularly weird about this one.

The old woman *smiled* at him.

Man, there were a lot of teeth there. (More than a while ago?) O'Hara thought: Now that's a crazy thing to think.

He was about six feet from her when she jumped him, teeth gnashing, clicking together like a hundred cold Eskimo knees. They caught his shirt sleeve and ripped it off; the cloth disappeared between those teeth fast as a waiter's tip.

O'Hara struck at her with his nightstick, but she caught that in

her mouth, and those teeth of hers began to rattle and snap like a pound full of rabid dogs. Wasn't nothing left of that stick but toothpicks.

He pulled his revolver, but she ate that too. Then she ate O'Hara, didn't even leave a shoe.

Little later on she ate a kid on a bicycle—the bicycle too—and hit up a black hooker for dessert. But that didn't satisfy her. She was still hungry, and, worst yet, the pickings had gotten lean.

Long about midnight, this part of the city went dead except for a bum or two, and she ate them. She kept thinking that if she could get across town to Forty-second Street, she could have her fill of hookers, kids, pimps, and heroin addicts. It'd be a regular buffet-style dinner.

But that was such a long ways off and she was *soooo hungry*. And those damn teeth were so big now she felt as if she needed a neck brace just to hold her head up.

She started walking fast, and when she was about six blocks away from the smorgasbord of Forty-second, her mouth started watering like Niagara Falls.

Suddenly, she had an attack. She had to eat NOW – as in 'a while ago.' *Immediately*.

Halfway up her arm, she tried to stop. But my, was that tasty. Those teeth went to work, a-chomping and a-rending, and pretty soon they were as big as a bear trap, snapping flesh like it was chewing gum.

Wasn't nothing left of Maude but a puddle of blood by the time the teeth fell to the sidewalk, rapidly shrinking back to normal size.

Harry, high on life and high on wine, wobbled down the sidewalk, dangling left, dangling right. It was a wonder he didn't fall down.

He saw the teeth lying in a puddle of blood, and having no choppers of his own —the tooth fairy had them all—he decided, what the hell, what can it hurt? Besides, he felt driven.

Picking up the teeth, wiping them off, he placed them in his mouth.

Perfect fit. Like they were made for him.

He wobbled off, thinking: Man, but I'm hungry; gracious, but I sure could eat.

Varney the Vampire

It is perfectly white—perfectly bloodless. The eyes look like polished tin; the lips are drawn back (to show) the fearful-looking teeth—projecting like those of some wild animal, hideously, glaringly white, and fang-like. It approaches with a strange, gliding movement. It clashes together the long nails that hang from its finger ends. No sound comes from its lips.—*James Rymer.*

GINA HALDANE
Grocery List

1 doz eggs
1 lb butter
  (I remember when we were first married how Bob loved
my omelets)
1 gal milk
1 lg box Whoopie Wheetsies
  (I wish the kids wouldn't believe all that junk on television. They keep begging me to get them this, get them that)
1 bottle Kalm-Tabs *(for stress)*
1 six-pack Macho beer
  (which will be gone by the end of Sunday's football game. Bob'll be dozing in front of the TV, wearing that old undershirt)
1 head lettuce
2 tomatoes
3 lbs hamburger
  (I remember when Bob said, 'Steak and caviar, baby—
marry me and it'll be steak and caviar all the way!' And now we can barely afford hamburgers)
1 pkg Sweetums disposable diapers
3 jars Bitsie-Bites baby food
  (maybe if we hadn't had three kids in three years, maybe then)
1 box Storm detergent
1 floor mop
  (or maybe if Bob had let me keep my job instead of

being
a broken-down housewife, I could have had a career)
1 Calorie-Counter's Meals for One
1 doz cans Lo-Lo Kola
   (I don't know why I try to lose weight. I'll bet she would
be eating all the time if her husband was seeing another woman)
1 bunch asparagus
   (I bet they think I don't even know about their affair! Well, if they think I'm going to let them get away with it)
1 box rat poison
   (damn them!)

LAFCADIO HEARN
Mujina

On the Akasaka Road, in Tōkyō, there is a slope called Kii-no-kuni-zaka,—which means the Slope of the Province of Kii. I do not know why it is called the Slope of the Province of Kii. On one side of this slope you see an ancient moat, deep and very wide, with high green banks rising up to some place of gardens;—and on the other side of the road extend the long and lofty walls of an imperial palace. Before the era of street-lamps and jinrikishas, this neighbourhood was very lonesome after dark; and belated pedestrians would go miles out of their way rather than mount the Kii-no-kuni-zaka, alone, after sunset.

All because of a Mujina that used to walk there.

The last man who saw the Mujina was an old merchant of the Kyōbashi quarter, who died about thirty years ago. This is the story, as he told it:—

One night, at a late hour, he was hurrying up the Kii-no-kuni-zaka, when he perceived a woman crouching by the moat, all alone, and weeping bitterly. Fearing that she intended to drown herself, he stopped to offer her any assistance or consolation in his power. She appeared to be a slight and graceful person, handsomely dressed; and her hair was arranged like that of a young girl of good family. 'O-jochū,' he exclaimed, approaching her,—'O-jochū, do not cry like that! ... Tell me what the trouble is; and if there be any way to help you, I shall be glad to help you.' (He really meant what he said; for he was a very kind man.) But she continued to weep,—hiding her face from him with one of her long sleeves. 'O-jochū,' he said again, as gently as he could,—' please, please listen to me! . . . This is no place for a young lady at night! Do not cry, I implore you!—only tell me how I may be of some help to you!' Slowly she rose up, but turned her back to him, and continued to moan and sob behind her sleeve. He laid his hand lightly upon her shoulder, and pleaded:—'O-jochū!—O-jochū!—O-jochū! . . . Listen to me, just for one little moment! . . . O-jochū!—O-jochū!' . . . Then that O-jochū turned round, and dropped her sleeve, and stroked her face with her hand;—and the man saw that she had no eyes or nose or mouth,—and he screamed and ran away.

Up Kii-no-kuni-zaka he ran and ran; and all was black and empty before him. On and on he ran, never daring to look back; and at last he saw a lantern, so far away that it looked like the gleam of a firefly; and he made for it. It proved to be only the lantern of an itinerant *soba*-seller, who had set down his stand by the road-side; but any light and any human companionship was good after that experience; and he flung himself down at the feet of the *soba*-seller, crying out, 'Aa!—aa!!— *aa*!!!' . . .

'*Koré*! *Koré*!' roughly exclaimed the soba-man. 'Here! what is the matter with you? Anybody hurt you?'

'No—nobody hurt me,' panted the other,—'only . . . *Aa*!—*aa*!!' . . .

'Only scared you?' queried the peddler, unsympathetically. 'Robbers?'

'Not robbers,—not robbers,' gasped the terrified man . . . 'I saw . . . I saw a woman—by the moat;—and she moved me . . . *Aa*! I cannot tell you what she showed me! . . .'

'*Hé*! Was it anything like THIS that she showed you?' cried the *soba*-man, stroking his own face—which therewith became like unto an Egg. . . And, simultaneously, the light went out.

RAYMOND CHANDLER
At Parting

Helped her lying in the nude
    That sultry night in May.
The neighbors thought it rather rude;
    He liked her best that way.

He left a rose beside her head,
    A meat axe in her brain.
A note upon the bureau read:
    'I won't be back again.'

57

'I tell you, Shirley, there's something funny about this place!'

RICHARD MIDDLETON
Love at First sight

(A) paper found among the effects of that unhappy madman, the late Stanley Barton)

It was Darling that did it you know, she looked so horrid. Not at first, of course. Oh no, at first she was lovely, but afterwards – oh! it makes me sick and crumbled to think of her.

If I had met Darling before her marriage it might have been all right. I had known Benham for a long time at the club, a big man, and I knew he loved somebody, but I never went down to his place till after his marriage, and then I met Darling.

Of course she was Darling from the beginning. I sat between them at dinner, and I looked at her and laughed, and he laughed too because he was stupid; but she kept quite still and her eyes were afraid of me. And that made me very glad. But he knew nothing.

Afterwards he had to go out for a little, and his big feet were hardly down the passage before I had kissed her. You see, I was quite sure. And she gave a little cry and shrank back into her chair, looking at me with funny eyes.

Of course she knew that she could do nothing – that she was all mine, because it had to be so – that her marriage was all a big mistake, because she had not met me before.

And I stood back laughing a little, because I knew that she wanted me to kiss her again, and it was nicer to know that, than to kiss her.

When her husband came back we had said nothing.

That night I was very troubled, because I did not want to share Darling with anybody, and I had no money to take her away for good. But I thought and thought until I saw things a little clearer, and I remembered a cottage that I had down in Surrey, among the pinewoods, where we could go.

So next morning after breakfast I told her that we should go there for a week, and then kill ourselves, together all the time. And I gave her a kiss and it was all settled.

Next day I borrowed some money from her husband and went back to town, and in the afternoon she came to meet me. I was quite sure.

And so we went down to the pinewoods together, Darling and I, to love.

All the days were very sunny and we would walk in the woods under the branches and love terribly.

And the nights were full of stars, and then I would go and dig our grave, and Darling would sit and watch me. I dug it behind the cottage where it was sand with great pieces of ironstone, and when the spade struck the ironstone it was not nice. But the sand was soft and I dug deep, oh deep! and presently we would lie together at the bottom of the grave, and the stars were a long way off. They would dwindle and dwindle until they went out, and we thought we were dead and grew afraid of the worms. But they did nothing and we got out again and found the stars.

And all day long we loved there in the woods, but at last the week was nearly done, and something went wrong, and Darling began to get white and afraid.

I said it was all right, but Darling was not sure, and cried, oh! she did cry—

But, of course, there was nothing else, for we had no money, and there was Darling's husband and lots of things.

So I said 'Come and sit in the grave and we must do it,' and Darling put her hands over her face and cried, oh bitterly, but I lead her along, and we both sat in the grave for a long time.

But the sun was so shiny and the birds would not stop their noise, so that I did not want to do it, and Darling cried all the time.

And I looked at Darling and it did seem such a pity, but at last I put the pistol in her hand and told her to kill herself, but her hand shook so that she could not, and I was afraid that she would shoot me first by mistake.

So I said, 'You are a coward, Darling, why don't you do it' – and there was a bang and I shut my eyes.

And Darling began screaming dreadfully, and when I looked, oh! she was nasty. You see her hand had shaken and she had done it all wrong. Such a mess!

I got out of the grave and she kept on crying to me to finish her, but I could not because she had the pistol.

And then I looked up and I saw her husband striding towards me and he had a big dog-whip in his hand, but I could not see any dog. But he looked over my shoulder and saw Darling, and stood quite still saying, 'Cover her up. Cover her up.'

I said 'What have you done with your dog?' but this was only an excuse because I did not want to go near her any more.

He did not hear me though, but he dropped the whip and suddenly burst out laughing. 'Damn!' he said, 'I'll cover her up if nobody else will,' and he got the spade and threw a lot of sand on her so that she was quiet at last, but I could not find his dog anywhere.

But he only laughed when I told him.

The Vampire

The British Museum authorities . . . condescended to place a bunch of fresh grapes on the sarcophagus and a cordon of police round it. When they returned they found the grapes withered and shrivelled to skin and seeds. . . . Things go on withering and shrinking. . . . They placed a live rabbit in its hutch on the sarcophagus and left it there for two days, but at the end of that time it had increased in weight. They tried a pound of beef and a small bottle of wine with the cork not drawn. The next morning, the beef was still fresh and still a pound, but the bottle of wine was half empty. On examining the remaining half, they found it just double strength, but of the same body—the constituents of the wine had gone, but none of the alcohol.—W. R. Hodder.

SINGULAR ATTEMPT AT SUICIDE

SINGULAR ATTEMPT AT SUICIDE
(Fact)

A few days ago a most extraordinary attempt at suicide was made at Newstadt by a workman named Brunheld. It appears that the man in question has for some months past been subject to most extraordinary delusions, which latterly were of so remarkable a character as to occasion some doubts about his sanity. On Thursday groans were heard proceeding from the upper story of an empty house, and for a long time the neighbours were at a loss to understand which some attributed to supernatural causes. On proceeding to the rear of the house it was discovered that the unfortunate man had made a futile attempt to crucify himself.

He had constructed a rude cross which he fastened firmly with ropes to an upright support and the window sill. Having completed his task he suspended himself by means of a rope round his shoulders and under his armpits. While thus suspended he drove a nail into his left wrist, thus fastening it to the wooden cross. This caused him such agony that it is possible he could not proceed with his task. His sufferings must have been fearful.

By the time he was released he had lapsed into insensibility. The poor fellow has been pronounced mad and has been sent to an asylum. Those in attendance on him say that his recovery is doubtful.

AMBROSE BIERCE
One Summer Night

The fact that Henry Armstrong was buried did not seem to him to prove that he was dead; he had always been a hard man to convince. That he really was buried, the testimony of his senses compelled him to admit. His posture—flat upon his back, with his hands crossed upon his stomach and tied with something that he easily broke without profitably altering the situation—the strict confinement of his entire person, the black darkness and profound silence, made a body of evidence impossible to controvert and he accepted it without cavil.

But dead—no; he was only very, very ill. He had, withal, the invalid's apathy and did not greatly concern himself about the uncommon fate that had been allotted to him. No philosopher was he—just a plain, commonplace person gifted, for the time being, with a pathological indifference; the organ that he feared consequences with was torpid. So, with no particular apprehension for his immediate future, he fell asleep and all was peace with Henry Armstrong.

But something was going on overhead. It was a dark summer night, shot through with infrequent shimmers of lightning silently firing a cloud lying low in the west and portending a storm. These brief, stammering illuminations brought out with ghastly distinctness the monuments and headstones of the cemetery and seemed to set them dancing. It was not a night in which any credible witness was likely to be straying about a cemetery, so the three men who were there, digging into the grave of Henry Armstrong, felt reasonably secure.

Two of them were young students from a medical college a few miles away; the third was a gigantic Negro known as Jess. For many years Jess had been employed about the cemetery as a man-of-all-work and it was his favourite pleasantry that he knew 'every soul in the place'. From the nature of what he was now doing it was inferable that the place was not so populous as its register may have shown it to be.

Outside the wall, at the part of the grounds farthest from the public road, were a horse and a light wagon, waiting.

The work of excavation was not difficult; the earth with which the grave had been loosely filled a few hours before offered little resistance and was soon thrown out. Removal of the casket from its box was less easy, but it was taken out, for it was a perquisite of Jess, who carefully unscrewed the cover and laid it aside, exposing the body in black trousers and white shirt. At that instant the air sprang to flame, a cracking shock of thunder shook the stunned world and Henry Armstrong tranquilly sat up. With inarticulate cries the men fled in terror, each in a different direction. For nothing on earth could two of them have been persuaded to return. But Jess was of another breed.

In the gray of the morning the two students, pallid and haggard from anxiety and with the terror of their adventure still beating tumultuously in their blood, met at the medical college.

'You saw it?' cried one.

'God! yes—what are we to do?'

They went around to the rear of the building, where they saw a horse, attached to a light wagon, hitched to a gatepost near the door of the dissecting-room. Mechanically they entered the room. On a bench in the obscurity sat the Negro Jess. He rose, grinning, all eyes and teeth.

'I'm waiting for my pay,' he said.

Stretched naked on a long table lay the body of Henry Armstrong, the head defiled with blood and clay from a blow with a spade.

65

AUBREY DAVIDSON
The Edinburgh Landlady

Now Jenny, bolt the outer door and trim the candle's
light.
Outside the wind blows bitter and you *must* stay home
tonight.
For just beyond the hospital, two killers idly lurk—
The name of one is Mr. Hare, the other Mr. Burke.
  Slung across their hand cart
  Rests a coffin box
  That carries pretty ladies
  Along to Dr. Knox.

Now Jenny, do as you are bidden for your own pro-
tection.
You know the Sawbones pays in gold for bodies for
dissection.
The poor souls go to Heaven from the house in Surgeons'
Square
To buy a flask of gin for Mr. Burke and Mr. Hare.
  Remember Mary Haldane
  With her golden locks:
  A pretty lady till she went
  Along to Dr. Knox.

Now Jenny, close the shutters fast and do not leave your bed.
I hear the church gate creaking and they're bringing out the dead.
It means the body snatchers are at their loathsome work,
And the best known of them all are Mr. Hare and Mr. Burke.
    One's a savage tiger
    And one's an artful fox,
    But both take pretty ladies
    Along to Dr. Knox.

Now Jenny's fast asleep and from the door I softly call.
I draw aside the bolt and let two shadows cross the hall.
My finger on my lips, I point the way toward the stair—
I get well paid for helping Mr. Burke and Mr. Hare.
    Such innocence and folly
    The Beast of Fortune mocks!
    For I send *all* my ladies
    Along to Dr. Knox.

ALISTAIR SAMPSON
Delighted Deb's Lament

What – has he shot himself for me?
Won't the other girls be shattered?
I'm sure they'll all of them agree,
One can't help feeling rather flattered.

ORNELLA VOLTA
Sergeant Bertrand (Fact)

He was tried at Paris in 1849 for having violated graves, after having been caught in an 'infernal machine' man-trap in Montparnasse cemetery, and was sentenced to the maximum penalty which was one year in prison. (Violation of graves is condemned by all legal systems, at least in cases where it appears arbitrary and unjustified. In the XVIIIth century, those dead found guilty were 'violated' by magistrates and ecclesiastics, according to legal forms.)

Unfortunately, as Epaulard would say, we know nothing more of the sergeant after his condemnation. His childhood and early youth are best known: as a child he had a distinct tendency to break and destroy all his toys with the result that his parents – living too early to benefit from Freud's theories – forbade him to play.

As an adolescent, when he enjoyed greater liberty, Bertrand began to cut up corpses of dogs and horses, and finally devoted himself to the dissection of corpses, without, however, having undergone any special training for this (he had studied philosophy at the seminary at Langres). His necro-sadistic passions came out fully during his military service. As he wrote himself in his confession (which was later published by Ambrose Tardieu under the title of *Extrait d'un manuscrit autographe du nommé Bertrand, deterreur de cadavres*): 'When a fit seized me, whether it were midday or midnight, I had to go off, there was no postponing it.' Dr. Epaulard has commented on this: 'All in all, Bertrand was a vampire just as other people are drinkers.'

RICHARD CHRISTIAN MATHESON
The Near Departed

T he small man opened the door and stepped in out of the glaring
sunlight. He was in his early fifties, a spindly, plain looking man
with receding grey hair. He closed the door without a sound, then
stood in the shadowy foyer, waiting for his eyes to adjust to the
change in light. He was wearing a black suit, white shirt and black
tie. His face was pale and dry skinned despite the heat of the day.

When his eyes had refocused themselves, he removed his Panama
hat and moved along the hallway to the office, his black shoes
soundless on the carpeting.

The mortician looked up from his desk. 'Good afternoon,' he
said.

'Good afternoon.' The small man's voice was soft.

'Can I help you?'

'Yes, you can,' the small man said.

The mortician gestured to the arm chair on the other side of his
desk. 'Please.'

The small man perched on the edge of the chair and set the Panama
hat on his lap. He watched the mortician open a drawer and remove
a printed form.

'Now,' the mortician said. He withdrew a black pen from its onyx
holder. 'Who is the deceased?' he asked gently.

'My wife,' the small man said.

The mortician made a sympathetic noise. 'I'm sorry,' he said.

'Yes.' The small man gazed at him blankly.

'What is her name?' the mortician asked.

'Marie,' the small man answered quietly. 'Arnold.'

The mortician wrote the name. 'Address?' he asked.

The small man told him.

'Is she there now?' the mortician asked.

'She's there,' the small man said.

The mortician nodded.

'I want everything perfect,' the small man said. 'I want the best
you have.

'Of course,' the mortician said. 'Of course.'

'Cost is unimportant,' said the small man. His throat moved as he swallowed dryly. 'Everything is unimportant now. Except for this.'

'I understand,' the mortician said.

'I want the best you have,' the small man said. 'She's beautiful. She has to have the very best.'

'I understand.'

'She always had the best. I saw to it.'

'Of course.'

'There'll be many people,' said the small man. 'Everybody loved her. She's so beautiful. So young. She has to have the very best. You understand?'

'Absolutely,' the mortician reassured him. 'You'll be more than satisfied, I guarantee you.'

'She's so beautiful,' the small man said. 'So young.'

'I'm sure,' the mortician said.

The small man sat without moving as the mortician asked him questions. His voice did not vary in tone as he spoke. His eyes blinked so infrequently the mortician never saw them doing it.

When the form was completed, the small man signed and stood. The mortician stood and walked around the desk. 'I guarantee you you'll be satisfied,' he said, his hand extended.

The small man took his hand and gripped it momentarily. His palm was dry and cool.

'We'll be over at your house within the hour,' the mortician told him.

'Fine,' the small man said.

The mortician walked beside him down the hallway.

'I want everything perfect for her,' the small man said. 'Nothing but the very best.'

'Everything will be exactly as you wish.'

'She deserves the best.' The small man stared ahead. 'She's so beautiful,' he said. 'Everybody loved her. Everybody. She's so young and beautiful.'

'When did she die?' the mortician asked.

The small man didn't seem to hear. He opened the door and stepped into the sunlight, putting on his Panama hat. He was halfway to his car when he replied, a faint smile on his lips, 'As soon as I get home.'

EDWARD LAUTERBACH
A Warning for Certain Victorian Ladies

*M*y seething heart throbs fast with stabbing strife
   As I touch each new girl, and slowly grip her
With iron clasp and draw my silver knife
Across her belly like a bloody zipper.
Not one would make a loving, faithful wife,
And each could frolic like a nightclub stripper,
So through the streets my murders will run rife
And I will nick each lovely whore, and nip her,
And slice her breasts and take away her life.
My name, you see, is really J. A. Cripper!

JOHN LENNON
A Surprise for Little Bobby

It was little Bobby's birthmark today and he got a surprise. His very fist was jopped off, (The War) and he got a birthday hook!

All his life Bobby had wanted his very own hook; and now on his 39th birthday his pwayers had been answered. The only trouble was they had send him a left hook and ebry dobby knows that it was Bobby's right fist that was missing as it were.

What to do was not thee only problem: Anyway he jopped off his lest hand and it fitted like a glove. Maybe next year he will get a right hook, who knows?

AMBROSE BIERCE
Oil of Dog

M y name is Boffer Bings. I was born of honest parents in one of the humbler walks of life, my father being a manufacturer of dog-oil and my mother having a small studio in the shadow of the village church, where she disposed of unwelcome babes. In my boyhood I was trained to habits of industry; I not only assisted my father in procuring dogs for his vats, but was frequently employed by my mother to carry away the debris of her work in the studio. In performance of this duty I sometimes had need of all my natural intelligence for all the law officers of the vicinity were opposed to my mother's business. They were not elected on an opposition ticket, and the matter had never been made a political issue; it just happened so. My father's business of making dog-oil was, naturally, less unpopular, though the owners of missing dogs sometimes regarded him with suspicion, which was reflected, to some extent, upon me. My father had, as silent partners, all the physicians of the town, who seldom wrote a prescription which did not contain what they were pleased to designate as *Ol. can*. It is really the most valuable medicine ever discovered. But most persons are unwilling to make personal sacrifices for the afflicted, and it was evident that many of the fattest dogs in town had been forbidden to play with me—a fact which pained my young sensibilities, and at one time came near driving me to become a pirate.

Looking back upon those days, I cannot but regret, at times, that by indirectly bringing my beloved parents to their death I was the author of misfortunes profoundly affecting my future.

One evening while passing my father's oil factory with the body of a foundling from my mother's studio I saw a constable who seemed to be closely watching my movements. Young as I was, I had learned that a constable's acts, of whatever apparent character, are prompted by the most reprehensible motives, and I avoided him by dodging into the oilery by a side door which happened to stand ajar. I locked it at once and was alone with my dead. My father had retired for the night. The only light in the place came from the furnace, which glowed a deep, rich crimson under one of the vats, casting ruddy reflections on the walls. Within the cauldron the oil still rolled in indolent ebullition, occasionally pushing to the surface a piece of dog. Seating myself to wait for the constable to go away, I held the naked body of the foundling in my lap and tenderly stroked its short, silken hair. Ah, how beautiful it was! Even at that early age I was passionately fond of children, and as I looked upon this cherub I could almost find it in my heart to wish that the small, red wound upon its breast–the work of my dear mother—had not been mortal.

It had been my custom to throw the babes into the river which nature had thoughtfully provided for the purpose, but that night I did not dare to leave the oilery for fear of the constable. 'After all,' I said to myself, 'it cannot greatly matter if I put it into this cauldron. My father will never know the bones from those of a puppy, and the few deaths which may result from administering another kind of oil for the incomparable *ol.can.* are not important in a population which increases so rapidly.' In short, I took the first step in crime and brought myself untold sorrow by casting the babe into the cauldron.

The next day, somewhat to my surprise, my father, rubbing his hands with satisfaction, informed me and my mother that he had obtained the finest quality of oil that was ever seen; that the physicians to whom he had shown samples had so pronounced it. He added that he had no knowledge as to how the result was obtained; the dogs had been treated in all respects as usual, and were of an ordinary breed. I deemed it my duty to explain—which I did, though palsied would have been my tongue if I could have foreseen the consequences. Bewailing their previous ignorance of the advantages of combining their industries, my parents at once took measures to repair the error. My mother removed her studio to a wing of the factory building and my duties in connection with the business ceased; I was no longer required to dispose of the bodies of the small superfluous, and there was no need of alluring dogs to their doom, for my father discarded them altogether, though they still had an honorable place in the name of the oil. So suddenly thrown into idleness, I might naturally have been expected to become vicious and dissolute, but I did not. The holy influence of my dear mother was ever about me to protect me from the temptations which beset youth, and my father was a deacon in a church. Alas, that through my fault these estimable persons should have come to so bad an end!

Finding a double profit in her business, my mother now devoted herself to it with a new assiduity. She removed not only superfluous and unwelcome babes to order, but went out into the highways and byways, gathering in children of a larger growth, and even such adults as she could entice to the oilery. My father, too, enamored of the superior quality of oil produced, purveyed for his vats with diligence and zeal. The conversion of their neighbors into dog-oil became, in short, the one passion of their lives—an absorbing and overwhelming greed took possession of their souls and served them in place of a hope in Heaven—by which, also, they were inspired.

So enterprising had they now become that a public meeting was held and resolutions passed severely censuring them. It was intimated by the chairman that any further raids upon the population would be met in a spirit of hostility. My poor parents left the meeting broken-hearted, desperate and, I believe, not altogether sane. Anyhow, I deemed it prudent not to enter the oilery with them that night, but slept outside in a stable.

At about midnight some mysterious impulse caused me to rise and peer through a window into the furnace-room, where I knew my father now slept. The fires were burning as brightly as if the following day's harvest had been expected to be abundant. One of the large cauldrons was slowly 'walloping' with a mysterious appearance to self-restraint, as if it bided its time to put forth its full energy. My father was not in bed; he had risen in his nightclothes and was preparing a noose in a strong cord. From the looks which he cast at the door of my mother's bedroom I knew too well the purpose that he had in mind. Speechless and motionless with terror, I could do nothing in prevention or warning. Suddenly the door of my mother's apartment was opened, noiselessly, and the two confronted each other, both apparently surprised. The lady, also, was in her night clothes, and she held in her right hand the tool of her trade, a long, narrow-bladed dagger.

She, too, had been unable to deny herself the last profit which the unfriendly action of the citizens and my absence had left her. For one instant they looked into each other's blazing eyes and then sprang together with indescribable fury. Round and round the room they struggled, the man cursing, the woman shrieking, both fighting like demons—she to strike him with the dagger, he to strangle her with his great bare hands. I know not how long I had the unhappiness to observe this disagreeable instance of domestic infelicity, but at last, after a more than usually vigorous struggle, the combatants suddenly moved apart.

My father's breast and my mother's weapon showed evidences of contact. For another instant they glared at each other in the most unamiable way; then my poor, wounded father, feeling the hand of death upon him, leaped forward, unmindful of resistance, grasped my dear mother in his arms, dragged her to the side of the boiling cauldron, collected all his failing energies, and sprang in with her! In a moment, both had disappeared and were adding their oil to that of the committee of citizens who had called the day before with an invitation to the public meeting.

Convinced that these unhappy events closed to me every avenue to an honorable career in that town, I removed to the famous city of Otumwee, where these memoirs are written with a heart full of remorse for a heedless act entailing so dismal a commercial disaster.

EDWARD BRYANT
A Functional proof of Immortality

M artin had just jotted the final formula for the conceptual breakthrough allowing the development of physical immortality, when the demon appeared.

'Too late,' said Martin. 'No need, trading my soul for a wish. In fact, I needn't give up my soul at all.'

The demon looked undisappointed. 'How about a freebie, then? Spot of gratis information?'

'No strings?' said Martin.

'None.'

Martin thought momentarily. Then he gestured around at the surrounding city. 'All right. How many of them will survive me?'

'None.'

'Perfect,' Martin gloated.

Then he saw vapour trails. Heard the demon snicker. Watched the dawn of nuclear fire.

PRISCILLA MARRON

My Dear How Dead You Look And Yet You Sweetly Sing

Florence under the floorboards did wonders for Wilbraham.

Made a new man of him. Shed several years he did. Light-hearted laughing days again he knew.

Was't going to caper off like Crippen. Not mad about male impersonators. No rage for the rolling deep.

Tap dance over her tomb he did. Delight fandango. Lissom as an agile lad.

Came, however, uncomfortable evenings. Songs by sad deceased. Visible in various sections. A wife in slices sings.

Haunting contralto she had. Real eerie. Sang better than Wilbraham danced she did. Cause connubial envy that can. Killing thing for vocally out-voxed fandango flinger. Hence histrionic hacksaw. Planks of heartfelt thanks. Sorry, Florrie. So long, Flo.

> *You mustn't imagine it's dead I am*
> *Though it's sitting without my head I am,*

sang Florence.
Wilbraham wasn't liking it one bit.

> *You musn't imagine it's drunk I am*
> *Though it's warbling without my trunk I am,*

sang Florence.
Enthusiastic Wilbraham wasn't in the least.

> *You mustn't imagine it's nuts I am*
> *Though it's knifing you through the guts I am,*

Florence charmingly carolled.

Wilbraham wasn't even listening any more.

Neighbours got nosy. Called cops. Wilbraham wantonly extinct. Hatpin through heart.

Florence *uxor intacta* under floorboards. No parts peculiarly missing. Songless. Hand sticking up though. Second hatpin in it. Poised for posthumous assault.

Sad moral story. Stick to divorce court. Take no hacksaw to your *hausfrau*. Direct route too drastic.

Employ intermediary. Practise do-it-yourself by proxy. Eschew fatal fretwork.

You'll be stronger longer the fewer you skewer with that gnat bat the matrimonial wife knife. Fact exact!

HORRIBLE CANNIBALISM

The New York papers publish a telegram from Kingston, that a Negro woman, of highly respectable character in the community, has been arrested on a charge of cannibalism. The accusation alleges that she has killed and eaten no fewer than twenty-six children, whom she had inveigled into her house. On a cursory perusal the natural impulse would be to consider the story an impudent falsehood. Highly improbable as this shocking intelligence may be, it is just and barely possible. Is Obeahism quite dead in Jamaica? It has been stated that "Vaudoux-ism" still lingers among the natives of Louisiana; and as regards Jamaica, a careful search through the Parliamentary Blue Books would reveal many extraordinary cases in which evidence was given of the monstrous orgies of Obeah, at which a calabash filled with rum and human brains was a standing dish. It would be worth the while of Mr. Arthur Helps to trace the parallelism existing between African Obeah and the ghastly human sacrifices offered to the Mexican gods described in his Life of Cortes.

FREDRIC BROWN
Nightmare in Red

H e awoke without knowing what had awakened him until a second temblor, only a minute after the first, shook the bed slightly and rattled small objects on the dresser. He lay waiting for a third shock but none came, not then.

He realized, though, that he was wide awake now and probably would not be able to go back to sleep. He looked at the luminous dial of his wrist watch and saw that it was only three o'clock, the middle of the night. He got out of bed and walked, in his pajamas, to the window. It was open and a cool breeze came through it, and he could see the twinkling, flickering lights in the black sky and could hear the sounds of night. Somewhere, bells. But why bells at this hour? Ringing for disaster? Had the mild temblors here been damaging quakes elsewhere, nearby? Or was a real quake coming and the bells a warning, a warning to people to leave their houses and get out into the open for survival?

Suddenly, although not from fear but from a strange compulsion he had no wish to analyze, he wanted to be out there and not here. He had to run, he had to.

And he was running, down the hallway and out the front door, running silently in bare feet down the long straight walk that led to the gate. And through the gate that swung shut behind him and into the field . . . *Field*? Should there be a field here, right outside his gate? Especially a field dotted with posts, thick ones like truncated telephone poles his own height? But before he could organize his thinking, try to start from scratch and remember where *here* was and who *he* was and what he was doing here at all, there was another temblor. More violent this time; it made him stagger in his running and run into one of the mysterious posts, a glancing blow that hurt his shoulder and deflected his running course, almost making him lose his footing. What was this weird compulsion that kept him going toward—what?

And then the real earthquake hit, the ground seemed to rise up under him and shake itself and when it ended he was lying on his back staring up at the monstrous sky in which now suddenly appeared, in miles-high glowing red letters a *word*. The word was *TILT* and as he stared at it all the other flashing lights went off and the bells quit ringing and it was the end of everything.

ALISTAIR SAMPSON
Essay

I am eight and Auntie Florence has just been to stay. All the family were terribly thrilled when we heard she was coming. Daddy made a wax image and stuck pins in it. I asked him what he was doing and he said it was terrifically lucky.

Then Mummy took all the springs out of the spare bed and I got scarlet fever and everyone was delighted. Daddy phoned up Auntie and said it was jolly infectious and he hoped she would still come.

On Tuesday she arrived at the station, so Daddy and Mummy tossed up to see who was going to be the lucky one. Daddy lost so he met her.

Auntie Flo wasn't very well. Daddy said it was 'the old ticker'. So I jumped out suddenly from behind the drawing-room curtains and held her up with a toy pistol. She had a fainting fit so Daddy gave me sixpence.

Auntie used to tell us stories about her operations, especially at lunch. Sometimes Daddy was so interested he hardly touched his food.

Auntie was awfully eager to find out whether the neighbour had false teeth, so whenever he laughed she used to put on her spectacles and study his gums. Of course that was a great success too.

Every time Daddy started to listen to a band on the radio Mummy murmured, 'Remember the will,' and switched it off. The only time Daddy laughed was when Auntie said she was enjoying herself so much she felt like staying for ever. It was a wild sort of laugh.

One evening, when we sat down to supper, Mummy said she'd made something specially for Auntie and no one else was to touch it. Poor Auntie died during the night and Daddy says he hopes she doesn't have an autopsy. And fancy; only yesterday Auntie was saying that she'd rather die than have another operation.

M A LYON
American Gothic

B efore the days of four-lane highways and people driving bumper-to-bumper, I roamed the dusty country roads across America. Bouncing along in my old Model-T roadster, I'd fling one leg over the left door, set the gas throttle on the steering wheel at thirty, and whistle my way across the open spaces of the West.

Some days I just smelled the good fresh air, rolled over the almost empty homestead acreage, and breathed the grandeur of the Rockies. And now and then an adventure would suddenly come over the horizon. I did not seek it, just enjoyed whatever unusual event came my way.

One clear sunny August day in eastern Colorado I watched the needle on my gas gauge slide dangerously close to the Empty mark. I thought, it's going to be a long, long, hot walk. I hoped the gauge was wrong.

Then silhouetted against the mountain on my left I saw a scantling shack about a half mile down the road. Pulling up beside the dusty gas pump that stood in front of it, I tooted my horn and waited. Nothing moved, not even the dust in the barren yard. There was stillness there beyond emptiness.

A chill slid slowly up my spine and prickled my scalp.

Out back a short distance from the house I saw a shed, so I got out and headed toward it. I was apprehensive, but I was desperate for gas. When I was about a dozen feet away a big rough-looking man, with three days' gray stubble on his chin, came out and walked toward me. He moved slowly, with deliberation, one foot set solidly in front of the other, and he had a hard mean look.

Under the bright sun the fresh blood that freckled his big square hands and spotted his blue overalls showed red and wet.

'Got any gas?' I said, trying to pretend I wasn't startled and nervous. This was not the kind of adventure I enjoyed. I could not avoid staring at those strong splotched hands, the fingers clenching and unclenching.

'Been killin' some chickens,' he said flatly. 'Ain't got no gas.' His cold gray eyes looked straight into mine and plainly said: Get goin'—now!

My legs wanted to run, but I forced them to walk without undue haste back to my car. Then I took his advice and got out fast.

That scene is as clear to me today as it was forty years ago. I have never forgotten it. You know, there wasn't one feather in that deathly still yard.

LIAO CHAI
The Corpse Rises

One night, four travellers, very tired, turned up at an inn in Ts'ai Tien, Shantung. The inn was full, but the travellers pressed the innkeeper to shelter them; and with much hesitation, he put them in a lonely house near by, in which his daughter-in-law had recently died. The house was lit by a dim lamp, and behind a curtain lay the uncoffined body of the girl. The four weary men flung themselves down on the beds provided, and three of them were soon snoring lustily. The fourth was not quite asleep when he heard a creaking sound behind the curtain. He opened his eyes and saw the corpse rise up, push aside the curtain, and approach. It stopped over the three sleepers and blew thrice upon them; the fourth, in terror, hid his head under the coverlet and held his breath. The corpse breathed on him also and withdrew. Hearing a rustling sound he peeped out, and saw that it had returned to its couch, and was lying as still as before.

Afraid to call out, the traveller stealthily kicked his sleeping comrades, but they did not stir; so he quietly reached for his clothes in the hope of creeping away. every time he moved, however, he heard the creak of the bier; and he dived under the shelter of the blanket again and again, listening all the time to the corpse, who came across and breathed on him. At last, a pause, followed by the rustling of the shroud, nerved him to a final effort. He put out his hand, seized some clothes, scrambled into them, and rushed, barefooted, from the house. The corpse jumped up, and although he bolted the door in its face, it chased him a long way, gaining on him until, in desperation, he dodged behind a willow-tree four or five feet thick. As the corpse darted to the right, he darted to the left; this went on for some time, until the enraged corpse rushed at him, missed him as he fell in a faint, and embraced the tree with rigid grip. At daybreak it was found, when the corpse was pulled away, that its fingers had bored into the tree like an auger. The traveller eventually recovered, but his companions all died of the effects of the corpse's breath.

From G. Willoughby-Meade.

DANNIE PLACHTA
Revival Meeting

G raham Kraken lay upon his deathbed. His eyes wavering upon a dim and faraway ceiling, he savoured the reassuring words.

'The odds are all in your favour,' the doctor said.

The bed seemed to tense beneath Kraken. Springs coiled tautly.

'Some day –' the doctor's voice rang with tiny, metallic chimes – 'medical science will have advanced far enough to revive you. Your frozen body will not deteriorate in the interim.' The chimes grew hushed. 'Some day science will repair your body and you will live again.'

Graham Kraken died easily and they froze his corpse.

He dreamed that he was in Miami Beach and opened his eyes. Blinking into the dimness of his room, he found a visitor seated at his bedside.

'Good morning,' said the visitor.

The stranger, Kraken noted, was an elderly gentleman with a bald head and a pleasant face.

'Good morning,' said Kraken in a friendly manner. 'Nice earrings you have there.'

'Thank you,' said the visitor. 'They're antennae.'

'Oh?'

'For the transistor radios built into my earlobes.'

'Indeed?'

'Stereo.'

'How nice,' said Kraken. 'How do you turn it off?'

'Don't,' the visitor responded. 'Speak up a bit, please.'

'I'm sorry,' said Kraken. 'I didn't know.'

'Nice weather we're having.'

'I hadn't really noticed. By the way, have they done anything about that?'

'Well, they did for a short time,' the old gentleman said. 'But they had to give it up.'

'Too many conflicting wishes?'

'I'm afraid so.'

'A pity.' Kraken glanced at the heavily curtained window. As he watched, the glass behind the curtains suddenly shattered. 'Oh?' he said. 'Riots?'

'No,' replied the visitor. 'Supersonic transports.'

Another pane of glass automatically slipped into place.

'I guess you get quite a lot of that.'

'Easy come, easy go.'

'By the way,' Graham Kraken asked, 'what year is this?'

'Twenty-eighty-eight,' he said.

'Well,' said Kraken, 'it has been a while.'

'One year is pretty much like another,' said the stranger.

'How about the money?' wondered Kraken. 'Did my estate hold out?'

'I'm afraid not,' said the visitor. 'I had to pay for your revival.'

'That was very kind of you,' said Kraken. He noticed the sunlight edging the window curtains.

He rose upon an elbow. The motion made him feel faint.

'Please don't try to move,' the visitor said. 'It's important that you rest for the heart transplant.'

'Oh?' Kraken leaned back. 'Is there something wrong with my heart?'

The visitor stood up slowly.

'No,' he replied, 'but there's something wrong with mine.'

ALPHONSE ALLAIS

Anything They Can Do . . .

L ittle Madeleine Bastye might have been the most fascinating and desirable woman of the entire nineteenth century but for one small, annoying fault. She was incapable of taking a lover without immediately being unfaithful to him. For most people broadmindedness means taking one thing with another; for her it meant only taking one man with another.

When our story starts, her lover was a fine upstanding young man called Jean Passe (of the firm, Jean Passe et Desmeilleurs).

Not only was Jean Passe a decent sort, he was also a credit to the Paris business world. So of course he was determined to do the honourable thing by Madeleine.

Not so Madeleine. She was unfaithful to him at the first opportunity.

Jean was heartbroken.

'But what has he got that I haven't got?' he asked.

'He's so *handsome*!' sighed Madeleine.

'We'll see about that,' muttered Jean.

Love is strong! The will is all-powerful! When Jean came home that evening he had been transformed into the most handsome man in the world, beside whom the Archangel Gabriel would have looked as ugly as sin.

*   *   *

The second time Madeleine was unfaithful to Jean, Jean asked Madeleine:

'And what has *he* got that I haven't got?'

'Money!' said Madeleine.

'Right,' gritted Jean.

And that very day he invented a cheap, simple, non-labour-intensive process for converting horse dung into the most exquisite plush velvet.

American manufacturers fought among themselves in an attempt to pour millions of dollars into his pockets . . . .

*   *   *

The third time Madeleine was unfaithful to Jean, Jean asked Madeleine:

'And what has he got that *I* haven't got?'

'He's got a sense of humour, that's what,' said Madeleine.

'Right,' grunted Jean.

And he headed straight for the Flammarion bookshop to buy *Pas de Bile*, the latest collection of pieces by famed author Alphonse Allais. He read it from cover to cover, and back again, till he was so impregnated with the spirit of this unique book that Madeleine could hardly get to sleep at night for laughing.

*   *   *

The fourth time Madeleine was unfaithful to Jean, Jean asked Madeleine:

'And *what* has he got that I haven't got?'

'Well . . .' said Madeleine.

She could not put it into words, but her blazing eyes said it for her. Jean understood.

'Right!' he cried.

If this were a pornographic publication, I could now tell you what Jean did next and we could all enjoy ourselves. Sadly, it isn't and we can't.

*   *   *

The fifth time Madeleine was unfaithful — oh, forget it . . . !

The hundred and fourth time Madeleine was unfaithful to Jean, Jean asked Madeleine:

'And what has he got that I *haven't* got?'

'He's very special,' said Madeleine. 'He's a *murderer*.'

'Is he now!' said Jean.

And he killed her.

It was about his time that Madeleine gave up being unfaithful to Jean.

JEAN COCTEAU
The Look of Death

A young Persian gardener said to his Prince:
'Save me! I met Death in the garden this morning,
and he gave me a threatening look. I wish that tonight, by
some miracle, I might be far away, in Ispahan.'

The Prince lent him his swiftest horse.

That afternoon, as he was walking in the garden, the
Prince came face to face with Death. 'Why,' he asked, 'did
you give my gardener a threatening look this morning?'

'It was not a threatening look,' replied Death. 'It was an
expression of surprise. For I saw him here this morning,
and I knew that I would take him in Ispahan tonight.'

"I was starting to wonder if you'd turn up!"

FREDERIC BOUTET
Pierre Torture (Fact)

This is a story about Pierre Torture, the headsman of the town of Colmar. His surname doubtless was bestowed on one of his ancestors by reason of his function, for the post of executioner had passed down from father to son for many generations.

His house, in accordance with the feeling of abhorrence associated with his sinister calling, was situated outside of the town, some way from its outer suburbs.

One winter's evening in 1780, while he was enjoying his rest by a corner of his fireplace, Pierre Torture heard a violent knocking at his door.

He opened it.

Three men, wrapped in heavy cloaks and with their hats pulled so deep down over their faces so as almost to disguise them, stood before him.

'You are the headsman?' one of them asked roughly.

'Yes.'

'You are alone?'

'Yes.'

He had no sooner answered than the three men threw themselves on him, and in spite of his exceptional strength overcame him. They then gagged and bound him.

They now bundled him into a roomy closed carriage which was waiting for them hard by, in the misty darkness, and got into it themselves.

They drove off at a quick pace, and it was not until they were already far from the town that the man who had already spoken to Pierre Torture addressed him again.

'You need not be alarmed,' he said. 'No one will harm you. We are taking you to carry out a sentence which has to be carried out. When you have accomplished this task, you will be taken back to your home safe and sound, and you shall receive two hundred louis as reward. But do not attempt to find out where you are going or who we are, and do not cry out for help or try to escape or we shall kill you.'

They then unbound him, showing him, however, threateningly at the same time a naked dagger; and the conveyance rolled on in the silence of the night.

At daybreak next morning they put a band round his eyes. The windows of the carriage were carefully darkened with blinds.

The journey continued all that day and throughout the following night and one more day, horses being changed several times and fresh starts made at a quickened rate. The three men and their prisoner ate in the carriage and slept in it. Pierre Torture, whose every movement was closely watched, could not tell in what direction they were travelling. It seemed to him, however, that they had crossed the Rhine.

On the evening of the second day the prisoner, his eyes still bandaged, was able to tell by the sounds made by the wheels that they were crossing a bridge: a drawbridge, apparently, for he could hear heavy chains rattling also. In a few seconds the horses were brought to a standstill.

A gate opened and Pierre Torture, guided by the men, got out of the carriage and advanced some yards. Presently they went up some stairs, and then through a succession of long halls, their footsteps resounding beneath the lofty vaults. The cold was icy.

At last they stopped and the bandage was taken from his eyes.

He found himself in a sort of huge crypt, hung with funereal black draperies and dimly illuminated by the light of torches. In front of him, against the wall, stood a row of stone stalls in which a number of men, garbed like judges, sat motionless. They were not masked, but Torture, owing to the nature of the lighting and to the distance, could not make out their features.

In the middle of the crypt, in the glare of the torches held up by attendants garbed in hooded gowns, a young woman was standing dressed in a long dark robe and covered by a thick veil. At her feet was a block of wood, and leaning against it a sword, which Torture recognized as similar to those used by executioners in Switzerland.

Then one of the members of the singular tribunal began to speak in German. He occupied the central seat, and seemed to be the president of the court. He said to Torture:

'You are here to fulfil your function. This woman is condemned to death, and you will behead her.'

Torture, who had been bewildered until this point by all he had been witnessing, now recovered his senses a little and protested. He declared he could not act as headsman in this way without the prescribed order from the authorities over him. He was an official executioner and not an assassin.

The president merely repeated his commands.

On Torture persisting in his refusal, the president—the while a great clock struck eleven—went on:

'You have a quarter of an hour in which to obey. If you have not accomplished your task within that period of time, it is you who will be the first to die. We shall find a more compliant executioner . . .'

The great clock ticked off the seconds . . .

'You have only two more minutes,' the judge said presently.

And an attendant handed Torture the sword.

The woman knelt down, turning back her veil as she did so.

Torture lifted the sword with a convulsive movement . . .

An instant later the woman's head rolled upon the floor.

Torture's nerve deserted him and he fell, fainting.

He was lifted to his feet, and with his eyes again bandaged, he was taken back into the carriage . . .

Two days later he was left at the door of his own house.

According to *Mantegazza* there exists a ghastly sport among vicious Chinese, consisting of sodomizing with ducks and slitting their throats tempore ejaculationis.

KRAFFT-EBBING

TOMASSO LANDOLFI
(Untitled)

Dear, oh dear. These breasts of mine aren't a woman's breasts, they're too tiny, too tender, I don't know. . . And the tips, they're just like a little girl's. . .

—Oh, come now, they're beautiful!

—And what about my hips? I don't have any, almost; you might say I'm nearly square from here down. Oh dear, oh dear, it's hopeless.

—What are you talking about? You look fine. Don't get such ideas into your head. Stop fussing.

—Why, just look at this face; I'v even got a kind of mustache. And my hair, it's so bushy. . .

—Now, listen, why don't you cut it out? Just relax, for God's sake. You're making me nervous, too.

—Sure, it's easy for you to talk, you're as hard as a pearl. . . And my thighs are a little hairy, too. Oh dear, dear, there's no hope, none.

—Say, you down there! Why don't you start getting undressed?

—Sir, please . . . how far ahead are they?

—Well, they're going pretty fast. It'll soon be your turn.

—Are we supposed to line up here?

—Yes, stand on this side—and as soon as you're called . . . In fact, there's one coming out right now.

—Miss, miss, how did it go? Are they very strict?

—No, not really. I mean, they are strict, but anyway I got through. Don't be so scared and above all try to act natural. Lots of luck.

—Well, get moving. Actually, it isn't your turn yet, but since these women over there keep dawdling . . . Go ahead. Hey, not both though, just one.

—So, kiss me good-bye.

—Yes, yes, I'll kiss you good-bye, but what about me? . . . Don't leave me here all by myself.

—Don't act like a child: a nice way to encourage me.

—Yes, you're right, I'm sorry. Lots of luck, but you've got nothing to worry about. . . . Oh dear, dear. Sir, am I next?

—Yes.

—Oh dear, dear. Sir, sir . . . tell me, what do they do if . . . if you don't get through?

—Why think about that now? Forget it.

—No, no, tell me. Please. I think I won't be as scared if you tell me. First of all, where?

—Why . . . here in this courtyard. No, don't try, you can't see anything from these windows.

—And . . . how?

—Well . . . it doesn't hurt. You'd think God knows what, but it doesn't hurt at all.

—Oh, now you might as well tell me everything; afterwards I'll be less upset.

—Well, it's like a big wheel, that is, half of a wheel, made of steel, it's very sharp and it turns: the girl lies on a board, naked, and . . . I'm telling you, it doesn't hurt at all . . . Oh, there's your girl friend coming out.

—Oh, you're back, my dear. Well?

—Let's not waste any time: they're waiting.

—But let her at least tell me. . . .

—Come, come, that's enough now, go on in. IT'S YOUR TURN.

A HORRIBLE DISCOVERY

On Thursday a nauseous odour offended the nostrils of the passengers and others in the station of Hermable-sous-Huy, near Liege in Belgium. It was found to proceed from a large black trunk on which only the name of the station could be found in writing. The commissaire of police was sought for, and on his arrival the package was opened, and in it was the body of a murdered woman, who had been cut up to piecemeal. Where this murderous package came from its not known.

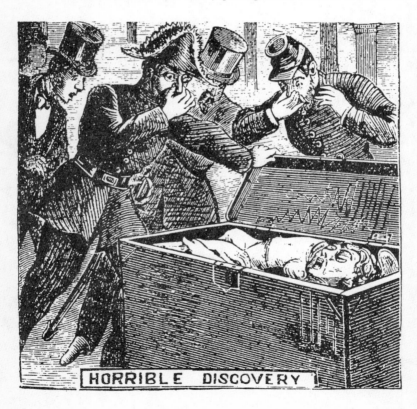

HORRIBLE DISCOVERY

GERALD ATKINS
The Midnight Lover

Women just can't resist me. It must be my special charm that does it, at least I've never had any complaints yet. I find myself embracing a different girl every night and pouring my warm passionate kisses over her with all the romance of Valentino and the cold, calculating seduction of Landru. They are at my mercy. God, I must be a handsome fellow. Success follows success as I leave behind me score upon score of contented female companions.

It all began last autumn with Clarissa. She was the first and truly the dearest in memory that I would recall. Oh Clarissa, my dearest, most affectionate love, what has become of you now? Her eyes glistened with the radiance of a thousand stars. Her lips were firm but sweet to taste and her skin was of the finest I have known. I loved her from the very first and my heart was heavy knowing that I must leave her for another. With her I learned the true meaning of love and that final goodbye almost broke my heart. But since that time there have been a thousand farewells and as many loves. Each one has offered eternal paradise but I have declined to seek the warmth of another. I cannot consider being selfish whilst there are so many who need my love and affection, a love that they would never find with another. I am their salvation, their only hope. Without me they would be just empty shells, unable to find satisfaction and contentment.

I love them all, each one as a complete individual from the rest, but I would never choose any one of them in favouritism to another. I have never given more time to one than any of the rest, nor have I rejected any who have called to me. I have always shared my love equally with each one as I know that some are capable of jealousy, and I believe that I am appreciated all the more for my fairness.

I have never actually attempted intercourse with any of them although I know that they would not object to it, and I have had several opportunities. My nature tells me that it would be wrong to take advantage of their love for me to indulge in this type of love. Anyway, in some cases members of their family are present and I would find it most embarrassing to attempt the seduction of a girl whilst under the constant surveillance of her dear mother.

Occasionally, I attempt to stay away from them for a couple of nights, but even as I sleep I can hear them calling me to their sides. I know I'm a fool and always give in to their pleas but I love them more than anything else in the world. Oh my little darlings I adore you all.

Perhaps the most confusing thing of all is that you never know who you will meet the following night, so I never under any circumstances make arrangements to see the same girl twice, and the thought of settling down with one of them has never entered my head.

There are certain setbacks however. Once or twice in the past some of my fellow males have become very jealous of my intimacies with these women. Perhaps it is because they do not have the charm and love that I have. For instance, last week they tried to put an end to our lovely acquaintance in a most primitive way. Fools that they are, don't they understand that their stupid methods cannot inhibit true love? I knew that it would have been useless trying to explain it to them as my words would never have pierced their thick skulls. So, instead, I waited until they had completed their futile retaliation against me and then under the cover of darkness I returned to my loved ones. Nothing could keep me from them. Oh my dear ones, my darlings. I have returned to give you my love!

The steel blade of my saw cut easily through the bars that had been placed over the windows of the morgue. Faster and still faster I cut, driven on by the thought of the glorious night that lay ahead. I'm here, my darlings. I'm here . . .

K C MANN

A Tale The English Used To Tell

The weary farmer stepped aside for the hunter's laden horse and asked the rider how well had been the day's sport. The richly dressed rider smiled showing teeth and replied that the game on the land was rich and tender. Seeing how happy the hunter was the farmer wondered aloud if he might share in the lord's luck. His answer was a sack thrown down and a cheery wave as the pale horse cantered away.

At home his wife's tears stopped the farmer's talk of his good fortune, and on opening the sack he found the body of his child.

FRANZ KAFKA
Before the Law

Before the Law stands a doorkeeper. To this doorkeeper there comes a man from the country and prays for admittance to the Law. But the doorkeeper says that he cannot grant admittance at the moment. The man thinks it over and then asks if he will be allowed in later. 'It is possible,' says the doorkeeper, 'but not at the moment.' Since the gate stands open, as usual, and the doorkeeper steps to one side, the man stoops to peer through the gateway into the interior. Observing that, the doorkeeper laughs and says: 'If you are so drawn to it, just try to go in despite my veto. But take note: I am powerful. And I am only the least of the doorkeepers. From hall to hall there is one doorkeeper after another, each more powerful than the last. The third doorkeeper is already so terrible that even I cannot bear to look at him.' These are difficulties the man from the country has not expected; the Law, he thinks, should surely be accessible at all times and to everyone, but as he now takes a closer look at the doorkeeper in his fur coat, with his big sharp nose and long, thin, black Tartar beard, he decides that it is better to wait until he gets permission to enter. The doorkeeper gives him a stool and lets him sit down at one side of the door. There he sits for days and years. He makes many attempts to be admitted, and wearies the doorkeeper by his importunity. The doorkeeper frequently has little interviews with him, asking him questions about his home and many other things, but the questions are put indifferently, as great lords put them, and always finish with the statement that he cannot be let in yet. The man, who has furnished himself with many things for his journey, sacrifices all he has, however valuable, to bribe the doorkeeper. The doorkeeper accepts everything, but always with the remark: 'I am only taking it to keep you from thinking you have omitted anything.' During these many years the man fixes his attention almost continuously on the doorkeeper. He forgets the other doorkeepers, and this first one seems to him the sole obstacle preventing access to the Law. He curses his bad luck, in his early years boldly and loudly; later, as he grows old, he only grumbles to himself. He becomes childish, and since in his yearlong contemplation of the doorkeeper he has come to know even the fleas on his fur collar, he begs the fleas as well to help him and to change the doorkeeper's mind. At length his eyesight begins to fail, and he does not know whether the world is really darker or whether his eyes are only deceiving him. Yet in his darkness he is now aware of a radiance that streams inextinguishably from the gateway of the Law. Now he has not very long to live. Before he dies, all his experiences in these long years gather themselves in his head to one point, a question he has not yet asked the doorkeeper. He waves him nearer, since he can no longer raise his stiffening body. The doorkeeper has to bend low towards him, much to the man's disadvantage. 'What do you want to know now?' asks the doorkeeper; 'you are insatiable.' 'Everyone strives to reach the Law,' says the man, 'so how does it happen that for all these many years no one but myself has ever begged for admittance?' The doorkeeper recognizes that the man has reached his end, and, to let his failing senses catch the words, roars in his ear: 'No one else could ever be admitted here, since this gate was made only for you. I am now going to shut it.'

GLORIA ORLICK
Hell Hath No –

Disdaining my heart, my lover left.
Should I be angry or be bereft?
Fury resolved in every way,
My darling lies beneath parquet.
Ah, 'tis tender and ever sweet
To have my lover—at my feet!

MARK TWAIN
The Five Books of Life

I

In the morning of life came the good fairy with her basket, and said: 'Here are gifts. Take one, leave the others. And be wary, choose wisely! oh, choose wisely! for only one of them is valuable.'

The gifts were five: Fame, Love, Riches, Pleasure, Death. The youth said eagerly:

'There is no need to consider': and he chose Pleasure.

He went out into the world and sought out the pleasures that youth delights in. But each in its turn was short-lived and disappointing, vain and empty; and each, departing, mocked him. In the end he said: 'Those years I have wasted. If I could but choose again, I would choose wisely.'

II

The fairy appeared, and said:

'Four of the gifts remain. Choose once more; and oh remember—time is flying, and only one of them is precious.'

The man considered long, then chose Love; and did not mark the tears that rose in the fairy's eyes.

After many, many years the man sat by a coffin, in an empty home. And he communed with himself, saying: 'One by one they have gone away and left me; and now she lies here, the dearest and the last. Desolation after desolation has swept over me; for each hour of happiness the treacherous trader, Love, has sold me I have paid a thousand hours of grief. Out of my heart of hearts I curse him.'

III

'Choose again.' It was the fairy speaking. 'The years have taught you wisdom—surly it must be so. Three gifts remain. Only one of them has any worth—remember it, and choose warily.'

The man reflected long, and then chose Fame; and the fairy, sighing, went her way.

Years went by and she came again, and stood behind the man where he sat solitary in the fading day, thinking. And she knew his thought:

'My name filled the world, and its praises were on every tongue, and it seemed well with me for a little while. How little a while it was! Then came envy; then detraction; then calumny; then hate; then persecution. Then derision, which is the beginning of the end. And last of all came pity, which is the funeral of fame. Oh, the bitterness and misery of renown! Target for mud in its prime, for contempt and compassion in its decay.'

IV

'Choose yet again.' It was the fairy's voice. 'Two gifts remain. And do not despair. In the beginning there was but one that was precious, and it is still here.'

'Wealth—which is power! How blind I was !' said the man. 'Now, at last, life will be worth the living. I will spend, squander, dazzle. These mockers and despisers will crawl in the dirt before me, and I will feed my hungry heart with their envy. I will have all luxuries, all joys, all enchantments of the spirit, all contentments of the body that man holds dear. I will buy, buy, buy! deference, respect, esteem, worship—every pinchbeck grace of life the market of a trivial world can furnish forth. I have lost much time, and chosen badly heretofore, but let that pass; I was ignorant then, and could but take for best what seemed so.'

Three short years went by, and a day came when the man sat shivering in a mean garret; and he was gaunt and wan and hollow-eyed, and clothed in rags; and he was gnawing a dry crust and mumbling:

'Curse all the world's gifts, for mockeries and gilded lies! And miscalled, every one. They are not gifts but merely lendings. Pleasure, Love, Fame, Riches, they are but temporary disguises for lasting realities—Pain, Grief, Shame, Poverty. The fairy said true: in all her store there was but one gift which was precious, only one that was not valueless. How poor and cheap and mean I know those others now to be, compared with that inestimable one, that dear and sweet and kindly one, that steeps in dreamless and enduring sleep the pains that persecute the body, and the shames and griefs that eat the mind and heart. Bring it! I am weary, I would rest.'

V

The fairy came, bringing again four of the gifts, but Death was wanting. She said:

'I gave it to a mother's pet, a little child. It was ignorant, but trusted me, asking me to choose for it. You did not ask me to choose.'

'Oh, miserable me! What is there left for me?'

'What not even you have deserved: the wanton insult of Old Age.'

ARTHUR L SAMUELS
Mass Without Voices

C raigus leaned over the bed of the dying violinist. On the walls
were pictures of his friend in more hopeful days, Guarneri
in hand, bow in position; higher up were a few pitiable memen-
tos—honorable mention in the Queen Elizabeth competition, an
autographed picture of Stokowski, but all irrelevant now. *Sic transit*,
Craigus thought. 'Please,' the violinist said weakly, 'you can't let
them do this to me, it can't end this way. Remember our pact.'

Craigus shrugged. 'I remember,' he said.

'Tell me you'll *do* it, please.'

Craigus looked at the picture of the younger man, eyes full of
hope, fingers arched nicely over a fingerboard that eventually they
had not quite mastered. 'I'll do it,' he said.

The violinist died gratefully.

A deal was a deal. Late at night Craigus lit the oven. When the
guage read 1,000 Celsius, he opened the heavy steel door and
carefully slid the molds into the flaming hot recesses. He locked
it securely. Ten minutes and a signal would let him know that the
molds were ready. After that would come the small boxes and finally
the large case. Big enough for a string section.

At the least the violinist should not have been turned down on
audition for the Detroit Symphony. That was really unfair, Craigus
thought. A judicious man, he added, it's merely restoring a balance.
I promised. I'm no Detroit Symphony; I'll come through.

Craigus went to the long counter. He placed the suitcase on top
and opened it, picked out a few samples, and laid them before the
owner of Strad Music Company, Inc. 'Beautiful,' he whispered,
'They should retail for three ninety-five each. You'd be foolish at
this price not to take all of them.'

111

'It's a good price,' the old man said, 'but I've got plenty of it I can't move.'

'Not like this,' Craigus said. He murmured something else.

The owner shrugged reluctantly and went to get a check.

Craigus passed through the doors with the rest of the crowd and sat in the last row, quietly. The Scala Chamber Orchestra, forty-five strong and true, drifted onto the stage. Each of the stands bore a fresh square of rosin; as Craigus watched, first the concertmaster and then the others absently rubbed it on their bows. Like children and mud, Craigus thought, string players could not keep their hands off fresh rosin. Like oboe players and their eternal reeds. They tuned deftly. The lights went down and the conductor entered. Craigus remembered him quite well. In his youth he had been a judge of the Queen Elizabeth competition. Of Brussels.

The Brandenburg Number Three. Craigus listened peacefully. The sounds began to go sharp and a cello squeaked. A violin made a rending sound, and the conductor suddenly let his instrument fall from his hand, a look of horror on his face that even at twenty-six rows Craigus could enjoy. Fine.

The odor began to waft through the hall. If it had already reached the last row of the orchestra, that meant it must be pretty bad down front. To say nothing of the stage. The La Scala players were trying to leave the stage, some of them holding mouths or stomachs. Not all made it. Craigus listened to the sounds of gagging.

Time to leave, he thought.

He stood and left.

'The pact,' he said to the sky outside . . . while inside, the audience was beginning to scream.

The pact, he thought as he got into his car, the suitcase on the seat beside him. Perhaps a little more encompassing than the violinist wanted; but on the other hand, since it worked so well, why stop with Detroit? There were lots of orchestras that could use good rosin.

Lord Dufferin's Story
(Fact)

One night during a stay at a friend's country house in Ireland, Lord Dufferin was unusually restless and could not sleep. He had an inexplicable feeling of dread, and so, to calm his nerves, he arose and walked across the room to the window.

A full moon illuminated the garden below so that it was almost as bright as morning, as Lord Dufferin stood there by the window. Suddenly he was conscious of a movement in the shadows and a man appeared, carrying a long box on his back. The silent and sinister figure walked slowly across the moonlit yard. As he passed the

window from which Lord Dufferin intently watched, he stopped and looked directly into the diplomat's eyes.

Lord Dufferin recoiled, for the face of the man carrying the burden was so ugly that he could not even describe it later. For a moment their eyes met, and then the man moved off into the shadows. The box on his back was clearly seen to be a casket.

The next morning Dufferin asked his host and the other guests about the man in the garden, but no one knew anything about him. He was even accused of having a nightmare, but he knew better.

Many years later in Paris, when Lord Dufferin was serving as the English ambassador to France, he was about to step into an elevator on the way to an important meeting of diplomats. For some unexpected reason he glanced at the elevator operator, and with a violent start recognized the man he had seen carrying the coffin across the moonlit garden. Involuntarily he stepped back from the elevator and stood there as the door closed and it started up without him.

His agitation was so great that he remained motionless for several minutes. Then a terrific crash startled him. The cable had parted, and the elevator had fallen three floors to the basement. Several passengers were killed in the tragedy and the operator himself died.

Investigation revealed that the operator had been hired for just that day, and no one has ever known who he was or where he came from.

RICHARD CHRISTIAN MATHESON
Deathbed

S ometimes, when it is very dark and still and the moon and stars send their light to this valley, it makes me want to cry. The peace is so elegant. Yet, I have seen such sadness here.

The blood and treachery that seek this place have always stunned me. Never frightened me but always made me wonder. All I can do is wish such things would never happen. Here or anywhere.

The people who try to help me come, too.

They bring their concern and their medicines. But I know it will do no good. Each life has its own time and I have had a great deal more than most.

I cannot always feel the pain but I always know. Such a helpless feeling. To empty bit by bit, hour by hour. It makes me sad sometimes.

My legs hurt most of all. I wish the people who try to help me could at least take away the pain.

But I know they cannot. I have accepted that. Still, I almost never sleep. I am very tired.

Strange.

To be so old and to feel death so close, yet to know thieves and opportunists want things from me. I suppose I will never understand.

Each wants something different. Each sees what they want to see. And it all comes and vanishes so quickly.

I have no answers to these things; only questions. Perhaps that is the point.

They will be here soon.

If only I could see as I once did I would know for sure.

Then again, it does not make such a difference to lose one's senses. All these years things have stayed very much the same.

The lovers come, hand in hand, to visit me, whispering as they stand near, making promises and plans. I always bless their love.

How could I not?

The old people who visit me alone because their loves have ended sadden me most. Usually their companion has died and I can see their loss as they get closer. I feel their pain when they come so near.

I have never had a companion, yet still feel their hurt and emptiness. I try to give them what strength I have. Maybe it helps.

The voices are almost here.

I hope there are children. I like them the best.

They always ask so many eager questions. And always about time. It is so difficult for them to understand how something they cannot see can change things. I feel it, too.

I especially love it when the children walk to me and their eyes grow big.

It always makes me remember.

And sometimes as they stand between my paws and stare up at my crumbling face, their sweet smiles make me wish I could go back those thousand of years in my beloved Egypt and be young one last time.

W. B. YEATS
'Magdalene'

One of Aleister Crowley's pupils was a young woman we will call Magdalene. She came under his influence at an early age and has since brought havoc to all she contacts.

One man committed suicide after falling under her spell. Several others were morally corrupted, and another young man who came under her influence, although he has now broken away, lived a life of seclusion in constant dread of her powers.

She drove his mother away and took over the ordering of his life so that he, a man of brilliant education and talents, became unfit for anything.

He woke one night after being drugged, to find that Magdalene and the man she subsequently married, were performing a death-dealing ritual with blood and candles around his bed, and they left the room congratulating themselves that he would be dead in the morning. By this time the woman was tired of him, but desired possession of his cottage and belongings.

She had brought him so low that he failed to report the mysterious death and burial of an infant of hers.

She sent for him on one occasion, and he fond her in labour – before the birth of the child she sent him away, saying her mother was arriving to help her. When she next visited him, she stated that the child had died, and she had buried it in the garden. The woman has a nine-year-old daughter who she wishes to turn into 'The Greatest Courtesan in England'.

She has a post with the BBC. She writes for certain magazines. Her tentacles stretch far.

The young man in question finally broke away a nervous wreck. He fears to answer the phone – or to admit visitors. He lives behind drawn blinds, and is constantly assailed with terrifying phenomena, to which his house-keeper vouches.

MARTIN GARDNER
Thang

The earth had completed another turn about the sun,
whirling slowly and silently as it always whirled. The
East had experienced a record breaking crop of yellow rice
and yellow children, larger stockpiles of atomic weapons
were accumulating in certain strategic centres, and the
sages of the University of Chicago were uttering words of
profound wisdom, when Thang reached down and picked
up the Earth between his thumb and finger.

Thang had been sleeping. When he finally awoke and
blinked his six opulent eyes at the blinding light (for the
light of our stars when viewed in their totality is no thing
of dimness) he had become uncomfortably aware of an
empty feeling near the pit of his stomach. How long he
had been sleeping even he did not know exactly, for in the
mind of Thang time is a term of no significance. Although
the ways of Thang are beyond the ways of men, and the
thoughts of Thang scarcely conceivable by our thoughts;
still – stating the matter roughly and in the language we
know – the ways of Thang are this: When Thang is not
asleep, he hungers.

After blinking his opulent eyes (in a specific consecutive
order which had long been his habit) and stretching forth
a long arm to sweep aside the closer suns, Thang squinted
into the deep. The riper planets were near the centre and
usually could be recognized by surface texture; but frequently Thang had to thump them with his middle finger.
It was some time until he found a piece that suited

him. He picked it up with his right hand and shook off most of the adhering salty moisture. Other fingers scaled away thin flakes of bluish ice that had caked on opposite sides. Finally, he dried the ball completely by rubbing it on his chest.

He bit into it. It was soft and juicy, neither unpleasantly hot nor freezing to the tongue; and Thang, who always ate the entire planet, core and all, lay back contentedly, chewing slowly and permitting his thoughts to dwell idly on trivial matters, when he felt himself picked up suddenly by the back of the neck.

He was jerked upwards and backwards by an arm of tremendous bulk (an arm covered with greyish hair and exuding a foul smell). Then he was lowered even more rapidly. He looked down in time to see an enormous mouth – red and gaping and watering around the edges – then the blackness closed over him with a slurp like a clap of thunder.

For there are other gods than Thang.

119

SHUTTING A WOMAN'S HEAD IN A BOX

A case of shocking brutality was heard at Durham on Saturday. George Robson, a miner, pushed his wife's head into a box whilst she was getting her clothes, and held her in that position some minutes then felled her, and putting her head between his legs, broke her jawbone. He then turned upon his daughter, twelve months old, and lifted her up by the ears. The magistrates characterized the offence as dreadful brutality and inflicted a sentence of six month's imprisonment.

ROBERT T KUROSAKA
A Lot to Learn

The Materializer was completed.

Ned Quinn stood back, wiped his hands, and admired the huge bank of dials, lights and switches. Several years and many fortunes had gone into his project. Finally it was ready.

Ned placed the metal skullcap on his head and plugged the wires into the control panel. He turned the switch to ON and spoke: 'Ten-dollar bill.'

There was a whirring sound. In the Receiver a piece of paper appeared. Ned inspected it. Real.

'Martini,' he said.

A whirring sound. A puddle formed in the Receiver. Ned cursed silently. He had a lot to learn.

'A bottle of Schlitz,' he said.

The whirring sound was followed by the appearance of the familiar brown bottle. Ned tasted the contents and grinned.

Chuckling, he experimented further.

Ned enlarged the Receiver and prepared for his greatest experiment. With unlimited wealth, his next desire arose naturally from the lecherous DOM deep within all of us.

He switched on the Materializer, took a deep breath and said, 'Girl.'

The whirring sound swelled and faded. In the receiver stood a lovely girl. She was naked. Ned had not specified clothing.

She had freckles, braces and pigtails. She was eight years old.

'Hell!' said Ned Quinn.

Whirr

The firemen found two charred skeletons in the smouldering rubble.

JESSICA AMANDA SALMONSON
Angel's Exchange

'Ah, my brother angel Sleep, I beg a boon of thee,' said grimacing Death.

'It cannot be,' answered Sleep, 'that I grant a gift of slumber to you, for Death must be forever vigilant in his cause.'

'That is just it,' said Death. 'I grow melancholy with my lot. Everywhere I go, I am cursed by those I strive most to serve. The forgetfulness of your gift brings momentary respite and would help a wearied spirit heal.'

'I can scarce believe you are greeted with less enthusiasm than I!' exclaimed the angel Sleep, appalled and incredulous. 'Despite the transience of the gift I bring to mortals, they seem ever happy to have had it for a time. Your own gift is an everlasting treasure, and should be sought more quickly than mine.'

'Aye, some seek me out, but never in joyous mind,' said Death, his voice low and self-pitying. 'You are praised at morning's light, when people have had done with you. Perhaps it is the very impermanence of your offering which fills them with admiration; the gift itself means little.'

'I cannot see that that is so,' said Sleep, though not affronted by the extrapolation. 'What I would give for your gift held to my breast! Do you think there is anything so weary as Sleep itself? Yet I am denied your boon, as you are denied mine; I, without a moment's rest, deliver it to others, like a starving grocery-boy on rounds. It is my ceaseless task to give humanity a taste of You, so they might be prepared. Yet you say they meet you with hatred and trepidation. Have I, then, failed my task?'

'I detect an unhappiness as great as mine,' said Death, a rueful light shining in the depths of his hollow eyes.

'Brothers as we are,' said Sleep, 'it is sad to realize we know so little of the other's sentiment. Each of us is unhappy with our lot. This being so, why not trade professions? You take my bag of slumber, and I your bag of souls; but if we find ourselves dissatisfied even then, we must continue without complaint.'

'I would not mind giving you my burden and taking up yours,' said Death. 'Even if I remain sad, I cannot believe I would be sadder; and there is the chance things would improve for me.'

So Death and Sleep exchanged identities. Thereafter, Sleep came nightly to the people of the world, a dark presence, sinister, with the face of a skull; and thereafter, Death came, as bright and beautiful as Gabriel, with as sweet a sound. In time, great cathedrals were raised, gothic and somber, and Sleep was worshipped by head-shaven, emaciated monks. Thereafter, beauty was considered frightening. The prettiest children were sacrificed in vain hope of Death's sweet face not noticing the old.

Thus stands the tale of how Death became Sleep and Sleep became Death. If the world was fearful before, it is more so now.

DEREK PELL
How to Write the Suicide Note

1   Use of the first person is generally preferred.

2   For maximum impact and credibility, always write in the past tense. (Example: I *was* a failure in business.)

3   If you are without family, friends, or even enemies, address the note 'To Whom It May Concern.'

4   When possible, use a typewriter. Far too many notes are indecipherable.

5   Keep a carbon copy in your pocket, in case the original is misplaced.

6   Do not concern yourself with the 'beginning-middle-end' rule. Just concentrate on the end.

7   Remember that these are your last words. They should be commensurate with your social position. They should reverberate in the reader's mind! Avoid such clichés as 'Goodbye cruel world' and 'To be or not to be . . .' Strive for the poetic.

8   Self-pity, slang and obscenity are acceptable.

9   If artistically inclined, attach a self-portrait.

10   Be brief. Nothing is more boring than a long goodbye.

ACKNOWLEDGEMENTS

Kingsley Amis, 'Mason's Life', copyright © 1972 by Kingsley Amis; reprinted by permission of Jonathan Clowes Ltd, London, and Random Century Group on behalf of the Author. Gerald Atkins, 'The Midnight Lover' from *The 11th Pan Book of Horror Stories* (Pan Books, 1970). Robert Bloch, 'The Model Wife', copyright © 1961 by Robert Bloch reprinted by permission of the Author. Frederic Brown, 'Nightmare in Red', reprinted by permission of Scott Meredith, Inc. and A. M. Heath & Co. Edward Bryant, 'A Functional Proof of Immortality' from *The Drabble Project,* ed. Meades and Wake (Beccon, 1988); reprinted by permission of the Author. Raymond Chandler, 'At Parting' from *The Notebooks of Raymond Chandler* (Weidenfeld & Nicholson, 1977), copyright © 1976 by Helga Greene for the Estate of Raymond Chandler; reprinted by permission of the publishers. Jean Cocteau, 'The Look of Death' from *The Book of Fantasy* ed. Borges, Casares, Ocampo (Xanadu, 1988). Roald Dahl, 'In the Ruins' by kind permission of the Estate of Roald Dahl. F. Scott Fitzgerald, poem from *The Notebooks of F. Scott Fitzgerald*, ed. Matthew J. Bruccoli (Harcourt Brace Jovanovich/Bruccoli Clark 1978); reprinted by permission of the publishers. Stephen Gallagher, 'The Mousetrap', from *The Drabble Project* (*op. cit.*), reprinted by permission of the Author. Martin Gardner, 'Thang' reprinted b y permission of the Author. Edward Gorey, 'The Nun' reprinted by permission of the Author. Gina Haldane, 'The Grocery List' from *Ellery Queen's Mystery Magazine*, reprinted by permission of the Author. Robert T. Kurosaka, 'A Lot to Learn' from *100 Great Science Fiction Short Short Stories*, ed. Asimov, Greenberg, Olander (Robson, 1978); reprinted by permission of the Author. Tomasso Landolfi, untitled piece reprinted by permission of New Directions Publishing Corporation, New York. Joe R. Lansdale, 'Dog, Cat, Baby' and 'Chompers' reprinted by permission of the Author and Vega/Agentur Luserke. Edward Lauterbach, 'A Warning For Certain Victorian Ladies' from *The Mystery and Detection Annual* (Adams, 1972); reprinted by permission of the publishers. John Lennon, 'Randolf's Party', 'Good Dog Nigel' and 'A Surprise for Little Bobby' from *In His Own Write* (Cape, 1964), copyright © 1964 by the Estate of John Lennon; reprinted by permission of Jonathan Cape Limited and Simon & Schuster, Inc. M. A. Lyon, 'American Gothic', from *Ellery Queen's Mystery Magazine*; reprinted by permission of the Author. Priscilla Marron, 'My Dear, How Dead You Look and Yet You Sweetly Sing' from *The 8th Pan Book of Horror Stories* (Pan, 1967). Richard